JELLY BEANS
IN LIFE

PAT

May the Jelly Beans in
your life always be sweet!

S16

by
Sig Schmalhofer

NOTES FROM THE AUTHOR

In this, the second printing of *Jelly Beans in Life*, the text has been re-formatted for easier reading.

Also, of note, the author has changed his name. Siegfried Hanover has been replaced by Sig Schmalhofer, a name that doesn't roll off the tongue, but is my real-life name; the name I'm known by, both personally and professionally. Moving forward all my books will be authored by Sig Schmalhofer. Siegfried Hanover is effectively dead! May he rest in peace.

For the latest Jelly Bean News, please refer to my website: www.jellybeansinlife.com

May the Jelly Beans in your life always be sweet!

Sig Schmalhofer

JELLY BEANS IN LIFE

JELLY BEANS
IN LIFE

CHAPTER 1

"The Ranch"

Neither the full bloom of stars illuminating a charcoal sky, nor the bulldozing of earth to the east, west, north and south, were his concern. The debates between freely enterprising home builders and small town traditionalists were a galaxy away from his simple mind. Trickle down economies, budgets, and deficits did not clutter his well-balanced head. His gait had slowed, his vision had blurred, and his heart beat a bit weaker. Nevertheless, as he sat with a relaxed confidence, he was without a glimmer of doubt, the 'Master of The Ranch'. Life counted him out in the spring of his life, so it was incredibly strange for him to now be in this position. Yet, there are miracles in life, and Charlie was proof. The longest of longshots became a beautiful surprise ending. That was the story of Charlie.

Charlie's home was carved into the side of a rocky hillside. The highest point of the property featured a bright white gazebo that glowed as if it were a lighthouse atop a craggy summit on the coastline. Not long ago the family gathered around the gazebo to release the ashes of Papa, their beloved hero and patriarch. It was Papa's wish to become one with the 'The Ranch'.

It was a spring morning, five years earlier that Papa sat with Charlie in the gazebo. Together, their perceptive eyes absorbed the menagerie of hues, smells and shapes that desert beauty embodies. It was then that Charlie's home took on the name, 'The Ranch'. Papa christened it, and the name forever stuck. There were no cattle, horses, hogs or even chickens on this ranch, but yet in some strange way, it was 'The Ranch'.

From the gazebo, Charlie's keen eyes could see the rock pathways that added structure to nature's splendor. Families of succulents and towering queen palms framed a desert tan, adobe styled home with red tile roof and a swimming pool trimmed with Arizona flagstone and a raised waterfall spa. The water in the pool was azure blue and inviting. At times, bullfrogs were drawn to the pool for a swim. These amphibian masters of the breast stroke swam freely before eventually being sucked into the filter's skimmer. On Thursdays, the pool man released them from their cage.

Since the climate was perfect for citrus, 'The Ranch' was the home of juicy fruit trees filled with lemons, grapefruit and tangerines. Naval and Valencia oranges were picked and squeezed for breakfast juice. In the spring, the evergreen leaves served as a canopy for newly sprouted blossoms that filled the air with a natural sweet-sour fragrance.

Towering above the citrus trees were populations of huge eucalyptus, pine, cottonwood, and sycamore. Planted in a lower grove were apricot, peach, and avocado trees. In the spring, fresh vegetables were planted and picked for summer salads. Tomatoes, peppers and cucumbers were mainstays that were grown in a large redwood tub. Melons and grapes grew lushly on their summer vines. Basil, parsley, and cilantro flourished in a raised planter.

The rabbit population was vast and ever multiplying. Blue belly lizards adeptly scampered on both vertical and horizontal surfaces. Countless varieties of cactus punctuated the landscape. 'Paddle Cactus', a delicacy of the Native Americans who first inhabited the area, grew helter-skelter at 'The Ranch', their arms randomly attached to other arbitrarily angled appendages. 'Prickly Pear' cactus grew in clusters and featured a red edible fruit. 'Blue Glow' agave sprouted a burnt orange bloom every spring and grew around beds of ranch rocks. A yellow carpet-like bloom capped the 'Golden Barrel' cactus, which made its home primarily along walkways.

But the most amazing variety of thorny growth was the 'Easter Lilly' cactus. Its columns, the diameter of a soda can, grew to a length of about five feet. When the cactus grew taller, it broke into pieces. The broken pieces rooted where they lay and grew anew. Through this process, the rocky slope of 'The Ranch' became the home to hundreds of 'Easter Lilly' cactus, named to celebrate the giant south-facing flower that sprouts from the side of the column, as if a child had glued it in place. A bloom, with its symmetrical white petals, was about the size of a car headlight. The spectacular sight would stop a north-bound Charlie dead in his tracks. Tragically, the 'Easter Lilly' bloom lasts but one precious day.

An artist's brush would struggle to match the unique and vibrant spectrum of colors that were displayed at 'The Ranch': bittersweet azalea, passion pink bougainvillea, dark magenta ice plant, amber bird of paradise, and daffodil margarita were just a splattering of identifiable color splashes.

No, this was not a home for the rich and famous. Realtors will always point to location-location-location, and this ranch was in Lake Mathias, not Malibu. Nonetheless, nature's splendor combined with man-made amenities certainly created soothing relaxation for mind, body, and soul.

Charlie methodically followed the trail down from the gazebo, keeping eyes wide open for deadly predators. Tarantulas crept around 'The Ranch' like cat burglars. The sight of the spider's eight hairy legs was more likely to cause the heart to stop than the tarantula's actual bite. Rattlesnakes slithered about stealthily. The brown diamonds tattooed on their skin were equally menacing, whether they were sidewinding or coiled for strike. Scorpions skillfully maneuvered their flat bodies around or under anything. Coyotes ran in packs and celebrated the catching of prey with a ceremonious high pitched cackling that broke the silence of any night. But none of these predators inflicted pain as frequently as the thorn of cactus piercing through skin.

A towering, sprawling sycamore tree marked the spot where the trail met a walkway. Papa had encountered a rattlesnake in that spot, but the six foot snake was no match for a feisty German, even if he was 80 years old. The side of a shovel was used as an ax that sheared the rattler's head. Papa buried it in that precise spot, in the shadow of that tree. From that point forward, the sycamore became known as the 'Rattlesnake Tree'. Charlie proceeded around the flagstone pathway that led to the front porch. He was neither scared nor cocky. Like Papa, Charlie and 'The Ranch' were one.

The front porch overlooked purple mountains in the distance and the sleepy town of Lake Mathias below. Lake Mathias was neither glamorous nor well publicized. Frozen snow-birds from the Midwest were drawn to the golf course resorts to the east in Palm Springs. Families, looking for new communities, moved from coastal areas to sprouting towns, like Corona, to the west of Lake Mathias. Tight budgeters, driving commuter cars down the freeway to offices or construction sites, found their new home in Sunnymeade. But Lake Mathias was sleeping through the Riverside construction boom of the mid 80's, much like Rip Van Winkle.

From where Charlie sat, he could see a steady stream of trucks taking materials to the jobsites located all around Lake Mathias. Flatbeds with bundles of lumber, bobtails with tile roofing, and chugging cement trucks traveled the road just north of town. Then came trailers filled with water heaters, cabinets, and yes, everything including the kitchen sink.

The owl that lived at 'The Ranch' paid no attention to the road full of vehicles or the homebuilding. He went about his twilight business on schedule. Every evening, right before sunset, he swooped through the air in big circles. After about a dozen loops he glided onto the upper branches of 'The Ranch's' towering cottonwood tree and hooted a wise owl hoot. To Charlie, that was the signal that the day was nearing its end.

Tucked away between highways going somewhere, Lake Mathias was going nowhere. Did Charlie care? Absolutely not! Did Charlie worry that Lake Mathias was just existing and not flourishing? Not a chance. Charlie loved to watch the flickering flashes of airplanes headed to Ontario, Orange County, or Los Angeles. But the flashes of light Charlie loved best were the headlights of Larry's Chevy Astro and Susan's Corvette. Those were Charlie's people, and the 'Master of The Ranch' loved his people.

In a sea of treasured gems, the town of Lake Mathias was never the cherished diamond; just another rock in the sand. Charlie didn't care if he was digging up a rock or a diamond, but a bone was always a tasty treat to find. Sitting on the front porch chewing on a bone, or even an old tennis shoe, was one of life's splendid rewards. Towards the end of the day, that porch served as a look-out post that provided a view of Penny Lane, the long winding driveway that led to 'The Ranch'. Penny Lane was so named by Susan in honor of her hero, John Lennon.

Charlie's ears spiked up like antennas receiving a signal. Yes, that was the sound of Susan's 1958 Corvette. The hushed rhythm of thunder from that jewel of a car could only be Susan. By the time she got to the top of the driveway, Charlie was already there. "Oh, what a good boy you are Charlie, yes, you are such a good boy!"

A singular ranch red rose displayed in a hand painted vase--that was Susan Schafer in her perfectly restored and beautifully manicured sports car. Brightly painted Signet Red with a splash of white carved on each side, this car turned heads. Susan would turn heads in any car but the sight of her in that Corvette caused temperatures to rise and ostrich necks to stretch just to get a glimpse at that eye-popping combination. The finishing touch was the, 'The Magical Mystery Tour' inspired license plate: 10-09-40, the birth date of John Lennon.

Susan knew Larry would be home late. Local plumbing contractors and their vendor partners had formed a trade association that met monthly. The meeting, on this, the eighteenth day of June in 1987, was tonight. She wasn't sure if any business was actually conducted or if it was just an excuse for Larry to get out of the house.

Susan recalled the love affair that had drawn them together. To begin with, they were born on precisely the same day and year, Jan 1, 1951. She was planning a project to create a scrapbook of the keepsakes that were the core of their love affair. A box containing memorabilia that was the heart of many delicious stories, was stored beneath Larry and Susan's bed.

They met in the spring and were married by fall. They supported themselves with minimum wage jobs, ingenuity and love. Larry worked in a plumbing shop, and Susan was a maid at Motel 6. They rented a three room house built in 1927, on San Nicholas Street in Ventura, for $125 a month. The tired structure had a tilted foundation that was high in the back of the house and low in the front. Since the toilet was positioned atop the downhill side, sitting on it was akin to a king on his throne. The living room consisted of one lonely piece of furniture, a ping pong table. Friends and family said the house had character. The truth was that only termites holding hands prevented its collapse.

Tuesday night was the highlight of their week. A local steakhouse served two steak dinners for the price of one, plus an 'all-you-can-eat' salad bar. They gorged themselves with salad and packed the untouched steak dinners 'to-go' for Wednesday's meal. This tenacious ingenuity exemplified their scrappy determination.

Crammed college classes were squeezed around busy work schedules. Viciously competitive games of ping pong were their recreation. But it was Larry's and Susan's burning love that made them forget that they were flat broke. They had no credit cards, no scholarships, and received no government hand-outs. They fiercely cherished their independence that was fueled by their fundamental ingredient for success that was a raging inferno in their bellies. They would prove the naysayers wrong and make it. They were steadfastly determined to get college diplomas and find rewarding careers. They would scratch and claw to make ends meet, and they would succeed.

That was Larry's and Susan's beginning, but that was now behind them. The careers they had immersed themselves into had brought new challenges into their relationship.

They were New Year baby boomers, now 36 years old. Larry always wanted to have children, Susan did not. She had seen too many screwed-up kids and did not want to add to that long list. She just didn't believe that she would make a good mother. Larry thought he might make a good father but Susan wasn't so sure of that either. Because their careers seemed to exhaust all of their time and energy, she wondered how she and Larry would ever be able to carve out the time and attention that children would require.

When Charlie was home alone, he was the 'Master of The Ranch'. When Susan and Larry were both at 'The Ranch', Charlie crawled into a safe, neutral corner. Susan and Larry had become cement trucks traveling in opposite directions on a one-way road. But, that had not always been the case.

As is the case in most marriages, relationships evolve. Sometimes passion is replaced by a comfortable complacency. In the case of Larry and Susan, the passion was still there, but too often misdirected. Still, there was hope. Every day, there were glimpses of the love that had drawn them to each other. Every day they still laughed and smiled. Unfortunately, the verbal arm-wrestling that they enjoyed in the spring of their relationship had now become a vicious competition.

Their opposite political views, influenced by their career paths, fueled conflicts. Larry was a conservative in the business world. Susan was a liberal and a teacher. But even on their worst days, there was an Olympic-like torch that their eyes shared when they met.

Susan loved 'The Ranch', but it scared her to be there alone at night. Charlie would provide comfort, but even on their worst day together, she liked Larry lying in bed beside her. She hummed a Beatles tune, "It's only love...But it's so hard loving you."

Charlie watched, with ears perked, every move of the ceremonious march to the bedroom. Susan, the professional, would be quickly transformed into a woman comfortably at peace with herself and the world. On hot days, like this June day, the pool was the next step of decompression. Her bikini was not as skimpy as the one she wore in college, but still, it revealed scrumptious peeks of a stunning woman. As her head-first dive crashed through the blue of the water, goose-pimples celebrated cool splashes of joy.

Now it was Charlie's turn. In years past, he would jump off of the diving board. But those showboating days were gone. With age comes dignity. Charlie pounced gracefully from the side of the pool. A splish-splash was followed by a doggy paddle to the steps and a shake that showered the Agave cactus. Susan now climbed into the waterfall spa; Charlie plopped on the deck beside her. Mesmerized eyes watched as the shadows of the valley gently melted into darkness. The wise owl circled his final loop before settling into his perch in the old cottonwood tree.

"Let's get something to eat!"

On nights like this, a salad would satisfy Susan's hunger. Charlie would feast on a bowl of chunky dry dog food. His appetizer, prescribed pills hidden in a squished ball of cheese, always made his tongue swoop from his mouth. Now it was Susan's turn. A lettuce base was topped with slices of hand-picked ranch tomatoes and cucumbers. A raspberry vinaigrette dressing added flavor, but not too many calories. A glass of chardonnay was the finishing touch. As Susan set her wine and salad on a TV tray, Charlie licked his chops and wagged his tail as if he was hungry. "Don't give me that look, I just fed you!"

As she walked down the hall, her hips swayed rhythmically, as both the top and bottom of her swimsuit were peeled gracefully to the rhythm of the Beatles tune beating in her head. She hung her suit in the shower and then crowned her lush naked body with a pink night gown that floated over her head and slipped down as softly as a parachute in a cloud.

She turned and stood before the mirror; aggressively yanking the wet tangles from her chlorine soaked, golden brown hair. Her head shifted sideways when a snarl became difficult. She stopped and stared at the mirror. Her brown eyes matched the color of her tanned skin. In a moment of self-validation, she shook her head. She was 36 years old and very much in the prime of her life!

Charlie, as if to confirm Susan's inner thoughts, brought closure with a singular bark!

"Let's go watch The Golden Girls!"

Susan's recliner, salad, and wine awaited her arrival. She flipped on the TV and propped up her feet. Her body melted into a comfortable position. The wine was as soothing as a Ventura breeze, the salad was a delight and the 'girls' were making her laugh. As Susan sipped and ate, she wondered why she and Larry could not be more like television couples—rarely fighting, always in love. But still, maybe they could figure it out. If only they could find a middle ground on the silly things that triggered petty arguments. Given middle ground, maybe they would laugh and love a little bit more.

After the nightly news, Susan and Charlie headed down the hallway. Susan's head eased onto her pillow as Charlie's body plopped on the floor beside her.

While Susan snuggled beneath her comforter, the 'Master of The Ranch' started snoring, as only Charlie could snore. When Larry was in bed next to her, the snoring was in stereo, but tonight Susan could turn away from Charlie and muffle at least a portion of the harmonic sound generated through nostrils. The windows were open. A refreshing Lake Mathias sage breeze blew gently through the window. The owl perched in the cottonwood tree hooted a deep bassoon riff. The cricket orchestra played what sounded to Susan like a Beatle's lullaby. Susan gently drifted into a deep Penny Lane slumber.

A ranch dream later, Larry arrived from his late night out. The shuffling steps were slow, not too sure, and relatively quiet. The night was as still and dark as a clock in a power outage. When Larry finally made it to the bathroom, he heard Susan's bark, "It's about time!"

"Hi Susan, you probably thought I was the ghost of John Lennon."

"Oh no, I would never be that lucky!"

Larry's retort was directed at Charlie, but for the benefit of Susan.

"Charlie, how is it that you're the 'Master of The Ranch' and I reside in the dog house?"

CHAPTER 2

"Lasagna"

L arry didn't walk, he shuffled, and at that moment, Laurenz Schafer was shuffling in the direction of his blue 1984 Chevrolet Astro van. It was amazing to watch Larry's shuffle. The net effect was forward progress, but positive net yardage seemed illogical because each sliding step forward featured a torso tilted slightly backwards and to one side.

Larry's Astro was a multi-tasking marvel. Its primary use was to haul sales samples and literature all around his Inland Empire sales territory. The same Chevy was also a cargo van. Sometimes the cargo was a load full of customers headed to a Dodger game. On other occasions, the cargo was the menagerie of 'stuff' that accumulated in the garage. The van, with 132,000 miles on its resume, was no stranger to the 'dump'. Larry guessed that trips to the dump accounted for five thousand of those miles. The Astro's paint had lost the metallic out of its blue. Even after a trip to the car wash, it looked and felt like a pair of old faded blue jeans. But that was okay, Larry didn't like new blue jeans anyway.

The year was 1987. Life was good. Certainly not perfect, but good. Ronald Reagan was president. That made Larry happy because he was a staunch supporter of the GOP (Grand Old Party) and proud to be an American. Sliced in half, Larry would bleed red, white, and blue.

As for the marriage of Larry and Susan, Larry steadfastly shrugged and said, "We started on a roller coaster and I guess we're still on it." Larry and Susan fell in love on the 'Rocket Jet' ride at Disneyland, in a downpour, on their first date. Larry still recalled the Beatles song that splashed through their love drenched heads: 'All you need is love'. Years later, when the music stopped, the rocket jet landed them in Lake Mathias, which became the home of a capitalistic Republican and a liberal Democrat who served on the town council. Their roller coaster relationship was wild and rocky, but never boring. Even viewed in high definition, the life of Larry and Susan Schafer would, at best, be a blurry abstract.

Charlie watched as a dry breeze blew a tumbleweed across the driveway.

Larry scratched his square head. "Okay, Charlie, if building cycles go boom and bust, and then back around, then why can't Susan and I?"

Susan's take charge voice interrupted the pondering, "Larry, Don't forget about Charlie's pills!"

An adage proclaims that opposites attract. Meet the Schafers! If Larry represented arctic freezing, Susan would head the committee for global warming.

Larry's brain was far from planet earth. A pipeline in his head was traveling to Sunnymeade and the big meeting he had with Town and Country Plumbing. The topic, of course, would be faucets, $PROH_2O$ faucets. Larry loved the fiercely competitive construction industry. He loved the relationship building that created longtime loyalties to him and his product. He loved finding clever angles to beat the competition. He loved turning assholes into allies and creating a team of loyal supporters. He loved $PROH_2O$ faucets and he loved to win.

Charlie squeezed through the doggy door, wet from a jaunt through the sprinklers.

"Larry! Did you hear me? You and Charlie need to go to the vet. Perhaps the vet can fix Charlie's thyroid and your amazing ability to ignore me with the same magic pill!"

"Okay, okay! Can I use your car? I have the biggest meeting of my life tomorrow and I don't want my Astro smelling like wet Charlie."

The answer was predictable, "Nice try, Larry."

Charlie and Larry loved the Astro. Susan just did not appreciate the value of a man's truck. The van was all go and no show but that was exactly what Larry liked best about it.

As Larry drove down Penny Lane, Susan entered the dreamy, imaginary world of 'Strawberry Fields', reminding herself that she really did love Larry. He was an absolute pain in the ass, but still, she loved him.

It was the last Monday in June in the late afternoon. Susan had just arrived home from a day teaching English classes to students whose school year would end on Friday. Her patience with 10th graders eager for their summer vacation was wearing thin. It seemed to her that Larry was more like a tenth grader than a man born on the same day as her. As she stirred a richly seasoned tomato sauce, she imagined that she was a pitiful number four in Larry's loves. Number one was his job. Number two was Jelly Bean Ronald Reagan and the rest of the GOP. Number three was Charlie. And then, finally, Susan at number four. Being number four in Larry's world was like winning last place in a hog-tying contest at the county fair. The fact that she still loved him, at times, made her question her sanity.

Susan was not a number four in physical attraction. Her shapes and lines were delightful. Her smile was inviting and her laugh was contagious. All looks and no personality? Not a chance! No, the Susan personality was not a number four!

When she was with a group of friends, sharing a drink and a laugh, Susan was like the basketball point guard whose job it was to keep everyone in the game by ensuring the ball moved around. If teasing was directed unfairly at someone, she acted the part of a referee who ensured unfair advantages were unacceptable. Amazingly, she did all of that with a giggle and a smile.

Susan's love for Lake Mathias led her to town politics. The previous November, she had been elected to the town council. She was well respected in town and had the mayor's ear. No, in smarts and power, Susan was not a four. She should never, ever be number four in anyone's life.

She kept score on where she stood with Larry, but only in her head. Her scorekeeping was a secret only Charlie knew, and Charlie was not spilling the beans, even if they were jelly beans.

As for Larry, he did not keep score in this kind of competition, but if he were asked, Larry would definitely rate Susan as his number one. Based on that, should anyone be surprised that Susan and Larry were on a roller coaster? Yet, Susan sincerely believed she was number four. And, in her mind, number five, Larry's boss, Frank Caparelli, was not far behind.

Frank plucked Larry from a small plumbing shop in Ventura, much like a baseball scout signing a sandlot player with raw skills and desire. With the right coaching, that kid makes it to the major leagues. That was the story of Frank and Larry. Larry was still a long way from his potential, but even at that he was breaking sales records. One of Larry's wholesale customers said he did business with Larry because he'd rather sell with him than against him.

John Lennon was Susan's hero. Frank was Larry's. Number five was tough competition.

The vet was in what the locals called downtown. It really wasn't much of a downtown. The corner of Main Street and Lakeview Road featured Sal's Café, a feed store, a four pump gas station, and a small farmer's market. The vet was down the street from Sal's, and did more business than either the doctor next door or the dentist across the street. That made sense because the population of animals in Lake Mathias far outnumbered the population of human beings.

Larry patted Charlie on the head. "Those thyroid pills are really starting to work. You're down to 135 pounds." Technically, Charlie was a chocolate colored Labrador retriever, but the truth of the matter was that he retrieved nothing. He was easily in the top one percentile in size for his breed. It was a rare day in Lake Mathias for Charlie to bark, and growls were as rare as a desert rain. The only injuries Charlie ever caused were to toddlers who accidentally got in the path of his powerful tail. The vet said that it was Charlie's thyroid that made him so big. Nobody knew what made Charlie so friendly.

"Here you go, boy." Charlie devoured the handful of jelly beans from Larry in one gulp. Larry figured if jelly beans were good enough for President Reagan, they were good enough for him and Charlie. Susan did not approve of Larry giving Charlie jelly beans. "What the heck, Susan doesn't approve of Ronald Reagan either." Unfortunately for Susan, the thyroid pills were not a magic pill to make Larry pay more attention to her. He frequently offered jelly beans to her, but they were always rejected.

Women puzzled Larry. "Charlie, a thousand-piece jigsaw puzzle with all the pieces colored Dodger blue would be easier to figure out than women. Marriage should include a book of instructions!" As if to say 'Oh Larry', Charlie responded with a mushy lick.

About halfway home, Larry's pager buzzed. "Damn, I need to find a phone. Frank is looking for me." Larry made a U-turn. He was typically good at finding operational pay phones that didn't smell like urine. It was a given that all public telephone receivers would stick to anything that touched them. Larry pulled into a run-down gas station. The phone booth did smell like a cesspool, but since he was running late, he entered, only to find the receiver's cord cut in half. Since the pumps did work and he was low on gas, he filled the Astro's thirsty tank.

Back on the road, Larry screeched to a halt in front of Lakeside Country Store. "I'm in luck! It doesn't smell like pee, and the phone actually works!" As Larry held the receiver with a rag, Charlie found a tree to initiate. "Hey Frank! What's up?"

"What time is your meeting at Town and Country?"

"6 AM!"

"Sorry Larry! Bad connection! What time?"

"6 AM!"

"Why in the hell is it that early?"

"To start the day off with a bang!"

"You and I both know that Town and Country has always been loyal to Alpha faucets. Do you really think that we have a chance?"

"You always preach that it's hard to get a base hit if you don't get into the batter's box."

"Alright, alright! I'll be there!"

"10-4 boss!"

Frank Caparelli was the mentor and friend who developed Larry into a clever industrial salesman with a knack for closing deals. Larry put Frank so high on a pedestal, binoculars were required to see him.

Frank was the western regional sales manager responsible for thirteen western states. $PROH_2O$ had a team of four factory direct salesmen working in Southern California. Those salesmen were paid a generous salary, provided with an attractive expense account, including a car allowance, and received a lucrative bonus for achieving goals. Frank considered Larry his top factory direct salesman and secretly had him tabbed for a promotion.

In the rest of the region, $PROH_2O$ contracted with Manufacturer's Representative agencies. Those companies were paid fixed commissions rates. This type of sales agency represents a group of non-competing manufacturers. Larger agencies might contract with 15-20 different factories. Manufacturers choose these firms carefully because the contracts are exclusive within defined territory boundaries. The success of a manufacturer within that territory is typically linked to the strength of the rep firm.

Frank's job was to train these rep sales forces and insure that $PROH_2O$ was garnering a disproportionate amount of their rep agency's time. Because of that, Frank was always on the road. He lived near Ontario airport, a central location within the L.A. market. His life was built around a crammed travel schedule that kept him single. Being married in Frank's crazy world would be challenging.

Because Frank spent ninety-eight percent of his time in the areas outside of the Southern California market, Larry didn't see too much of him. Other than their monthly golf outing, their time together was limited.

Larry again addressed Charlie, "Frank is making the call on Town and Country with me. When we close this deal I'm sure to get the attention of the home office!"

As the Astro pulled into the driveway, Larry quickly shifted into Susan gear. As they walked through the front door, Susan gave Larry the 'Susan Look'. In turbulent moments like this, Charlie was smart enough to crawl into his bed in a neutral corner to watch the inevitable conflict. He wondered if he really wanted to be the master of this ranch. Yes, Charlie smelled trouble. His keen brown eyes agreed. His tail sucked beneath him without a trace. He sniffed trouble and trouble was coming.

Larry recognized an angry Susan and made a defensive move to extinguish the dynamite before it exploded, "I don't know what I did, but I'm sorry!"

"Surely even you know the answer to that question!"

"I guess I'm late."

"Because you asked me to cook you Lasagna, I've spent the afternoon in the kitchen. I told you it would be ready at 6. Then you daydream and fiddle around in the garage most of the day and then, finally you go to the vet and God only knows why it took you two hours to do a 45 minute chore. I know your Astro shakes when you push it past 45 MPH, but it would be nice if you remembered the simplest of simple considerations!"

"Give me a break. I wasn't fiddling in the garage. I was getting my faucet samples clean and polished. And then, when I was coming back from the vet, Frank paged me. God knows, it isn't easy to find an operating pay phone in this corner of the world. Anyway, the good news is that Frank is joining me to the Town and Country Plumbing meeting."

"Why in the world would I be interested in Town and Country? Construction people are giving me a fit because they're unhappy with the moratorium we have in this town!"

"I agree that construction people want to work on projects. That's how they make a living. But projects also generate revenue. Lake Mathias roads, schools, and parks are all worn slick. Construction would create the money to improve our infrastructure. Government, small or large, can prevent progress. There's no evidence of any improvement in anything since the moratorium took effect. Meanwhile, we've got the so-called 'disadvantaged' standing on street corners receiving government handouts. Building would open up jobs for them. Put a shovel in their hands so they can dig a trench. Maybe, just maybe, they'll dig their way out of the hole they've dug for themselves. I dug plenty of ditches when I worked for Big Ben in Ventura; it sure as hell didn't hurt me!"

"If you're so darn smart, why don't you go into politics? Oops, let me take that back. The last thing we need around here is the narrow-minded ideas that you and the GOP are passing around as prosperity. What makes you think that builders would generously give back to the community? Business people only spend money when government puts a gun to their head. That trickle-down nonsense being thrown around by your movie star president will ruin this country. And let me tell you one more thing. Your boss, Frank, beeps and you jump. How about me? Did you respond to my page?"

Larry looked at his pager. The Ranch's home number popped up. Damn! He had done it again. He had brought the rage of Susan into play without intending to. She was absolutely right! He had screwed up! Big time!

"I am so...so sorry! I have no idea what to say or how to make it up to you, but let me give it a try! Is there any way I can interest you in a handful of jelly beans?"

"Absolutely not!"

"Then let's share a bottle of wine on the deck watching Mr. Owl add closure to the day while we enjoy the best lasagna in the English speaking world!"

Even Susan couldn't turn down that offer.

Charlie took a deep, deep breath, snorted, and exhaled with relief. Yes, there would be leftovers after all!

CHAPTER 3

"The Buckle"

The year was 1987. There would be 30,000 new homes built in Southern California's Riverside County that year. Tradesmen like framers, electricians, and plumbers were in high demand. Wholesale distributors to the trades were equally busy filling material requisitions and placing orders with factories working around the clock to keep the supply chain moving. Government workers feverishly raced with builders, futilely intent on having the infrastructure needed to serve the surges in population, in place.

Home building super-charged the local economy. During construction recessions, the sizzle on the stoves of Inland Empire restaurants is diminished. Furniture and hardware stores don't benefit from credit card crazy homeowners buying sofas, refrigerators, and lawn mowers.

But in the summer of 1987, building was booming at a sonic pace. Life was good. Larry agreed. In healthy economies, all governments, from the smallest of small to the biggest of big doing business on Pennsylvania Avenue, begin to plan their agendas and budgets. Bigger paychecks and frantic cash registers create income and sales tax revenue for the government. Those tax dollars funnel into the hands of politicians, who find ways to re-distribute those dollars into causes sure to win them re-election. When construction booms and the income stream flows like the Colorado River, politicians are happy.

When construction slows, drought conditions turn cash-flow streams into dry riverbeds and elected officials give speeches that take the form of a forty-mile detour. When pressed for explanations and solutions, savvy politicians resort to attacking their colleagues on the other side of the aisle.

But, that was not the case in 1987. The boom was on. Companies like PROH$_2$O were developing strategies sure to get them their fair share of the business. Or better yet, a disproportionate share. Larry Schafer was one of those people driven to make his mark, and now was the time.

His head was spinning like an air traffic controller at rush hour. No, he was not landing airplanes, but he was engineering the conversion of America's largest plumbing contractor to his product. That was enough to keep him from getting even a smidgeon of sleep. He was already in the shower when the alarm clock rang at 4:30 AM. As Susan rolled across the bed to slam off the clock, she growled, "Thanks for the wake-up call, Larry!"

At the shriek of the first buzz, Charlie buried his head under his Charlie-sized pillow and plopped his paws on his ears to muffle the aggravating attack on his far-away dreams. By the time Larry got out of the shower, Susan was happily in her dreams, in a deep sleepy sleep.

Noting his jelly bean inventory was low, Larry went to the pantry and re-loaded, stuffing a bag into his right pocket. He hoped the Jelly Beans in his life would be particularly sweet on this, his big day to make a huge mark.

He opened the van's back hatch and verified that he had packed all the items on his list: catalogs, literature, samples, valve cut-away, price sheets, business cards, polishing rag, PROH$_2$O baseball caps, slide projector, and slide carousel of a PROH$_2$O factory tour. Larry mumbled the first rule of selling that Frank had taught him, "You only have one chance to make a first impression!"

Larry slid across the tired seat and paused a moment. The time was 5 AM. The appointment with Ernie Nelson, the purchasing agent for Town and Country Plumbing, was at six. Although it was just a thirty minute drive to Town and Country, Larry remembered to add fifteen minutes to the drive time to accommodate 'Standard Frank Time'. Frank had drilled into Larry the importance of being to the customer at least fifteen minutes early. Larry then added an additional fifteen minutes so he would be on 'Standard Frank Time' for his pre-meeting with Frank.

As a charged and confident Larry crept down sleepy Penny Lane in his Astro, he suddenly remembered that he had forgotten to confirm the meeting place with Frank.

After frantically reversing back up the driveway, Larry burst through the back door. He yanked the phone receiver and pounded the numbers to Frank's house. Charlie was not happy as he had now been awakened twice. After Larry gave him a handful of jelly beans, his tail signaled a U-turn and he groggily headed back to bed.

"Frank, this is Larry."

"No shit, Larry, who else would be calling me at five o'clock in the morning? Okay, be quick about it!"

"About what?"

"The directions! Why the hell do you think I paged you? I need the directions!"

Larry missed the beep of the pager. "Good thing I remembered what I forgot to remember, right Frank?"

"As usual, you are making no sense whatsoever!"

Larry took a deep gulping breath and steadied his shaking hands. "Take the 215 south to the expressway and head east past the Flier's Café. Go about a mile. Turn right on the second dirt road, just past the end of the white split-rail fence. When you come to a fork, veer to the right and follow it out past the first barn and then out to the next one. I'll meet you in front of the second barn."

"You're damn lucky that I can translate your cryptic rambling."

"What?"

"Never mind, Larry! Get your ass moving! We're late! And you know, I don't tolerate 'late'!"

A frantic moment later, Larry was hurrying down Penny Lane. It was 5:10 and there was time to make up. He cursed himself for neglecting to give Frank the directions to Town and Country. "Okay Larry, you messed up, but it's going to be alright. Frank Time will save us, I hope!"

Town and Country Plumbing was headquartered in Sunnymeade, a dusty corner of the county that stood in the shadow of March Air Force Base. Because of their connection to Cedar Wood Developers, the largest homebuilder in the building boom, Town and Country was easily the highest volume plumbing contractor in Riverside County, and perhaps the nation. Larry's research indicated that Town and Country had contracts to do the plumbing on 12,000 houses in 1987; extrapolating to 84,000 faucets; making them a two million-dollar faucet account. Larry had done the numbers in his head, seemingly, 84,000 times and always came up with same answer. Astoundingly, Town and Country Plumbing alone represented twice the business of Larry's entire territory. Larry's mission, to convert the business, would begin today!

Larry sped through the thick of the pre-dawn darkness. The forever drive had only moved the hand of the clock 18 minutes. He whizzed past the Flier's Café. In the still of the morning, the lights were on and it was open for business. The Astro slowed when it came to the split-rail fence and then turned sharply onto the second dusty road, just as planned. Larry took the fork to the right, passed the first barn and screeched to a halt at the second barn. The time was 5:40. Frank rolled in right behind him.

"There's not much parking up further, so jump in with me!"

Frank Caparelli settled into his seat and smiled. "Good morning, Larry!"

Ahead of them, they could see a village of barns surrounded by pick-up trucks and bobtail stake-bed delivery vehicles. In the fenced-in gas pipe fabrication yard, oil was squirting into the jaws of pipe machines that were cutting and threading steel gas pipe that would be pre-assembled, bundled, and hauled to job sites. A second yard featured black plastic sewer piping that would be cut and glued to fittings. Those fabrications would also be shipped to jobs.

As Larry and Frank drove through the Town and Country Plumbing campus, it became clear that long before it was a plumbing shop, it was a farm. An old tractor, or at least what was left of it, was sadly positioned in the very spot where it had died from exhaustion, likely about 20 years ago. A horse trailer sat on one tire in soggy ground.

They made a hard right turn, which put them directly in front of the corporate headquarters. The barn that served as the main office was freshly painted. On the siding, in wood carved letters were the words, 'Town and Country Plumbing'.

The time was 5:55. As soon as the Astro stopped, the hatch opened. Larry scrambled for a 3-ring binder, literature, samples, price sheet, and PROH$_2$O caps. He took one big step towards the main entrance when Frank interceded, "Larry! Stop!"

"Yes, sir!"

"You've only get one chance to make a first impression."

"Yes, sir!"

"Let me see what you've got together. I want to take a peek at the samples."

Larry opened his black sample case. It looked like a travel suitcase, but when opened, the case had samples stuffed into foam pockets on both sides. Frank removed one of the faucets and inspected it. "Looks good, Larry. Looks like you just polished these puppies. Plus, you remembered your black velvet display cloth. Our faucets look like fine jewelry when you sit them on that background. If we get into a hot and heavy meeting, we'll bring in the slide presentation. You were smart to leave it in the car for now. You've got business cards, right?"

"I will, as soon as I retrieve some from my van!"

Larry scrambled back into the Astro and grabbed a handful of cards.

"OK, Larry, who are we here to see?"

"Ernie Nelson."

"He's the owner?"

"No, he's the buyer!"

"Who's the owner?"

"Mr. Starr, but he lets his people run the show!"

Larry and Frank proceeded, walking through the entrance of the largest plumbing contractor in the west. The oversized reception desk was unoccupied, but not the front office. Confident, controlling job superintendents dressed in jeans, plaid shirts and boots scampered about with blueprints in their arms or walkie-talkies in their hands. They were reading off material lists, giving directions to jobs, reading the measurement of a toilet rough-in, or trying to explain an inevitable screw-up. The lobby was a textbook example of organized confusion.

Larry and Frank felt like a stalled car in the fast lane of the freeway, at rush hour. Finally, they were greeted by a sympathizing soul who was probably just trying to tow them out of harm's way. "Who are you guys here to see?"

Larry confidently spoke up. "We have a 6 o'clock appointment with Ernie Nelson!"

After a hardy laugh, the man replied, "It looks like my man Ernie caught you!"

"I'm sorry, I don't understand. My name's Larry Schafer and this is my boss, Frank Caparelli. We're here to talk to Ernie about PROH$_2$O faucets. Here's my card!"

"Well, fellas, when Ernie has no interest in talking to a salesman, he tells them to show up at six. Ernie usually doesn't get to the office until about 7:30!"

The exhilaration of the big meeting had been slammed to the ground. Larry tempered his outrage, replying, "That's disappointing. Damn disappointing!"

The man reached out, shook hands, and introduced himself. "My name is Red." Larry looked at Red's belt buckle. The letters R and S were formed into a star shape fitted into the rectangular buckle. Red's cowboy hat featured the words 'Town and Country' embroidered on the face. Red handed each of them a card.

"Gentlemen, thank you for visiting us. I'm sorry for your trouble. I don't approve of the game that Ernie played on you, but I'm sorry to tell you that we have absolutely no interest, whatsoever, in changing faucet lines. For ten years, every faucet this company has purchased and installed has been manufactured by Alpha. We are an Alpha shop! Period!"

Larry glanced at the business card and celebrated quietly. Red was the owner. They didn't have a meeting with Ernie, but they did meet the owner of Town and Country Plumbing. "It's a pleasure to meet you, Red. You have quite an operation here. We are very impressed. We'd really like to learn more about your business and how you've become so successful!"

"I admire your spunk, but I've got a busy day ahead of me. Perhaps we'll meet again!" Red shook hands and walked down a long hallway. Larry and Frank stood there like the old tractor that they passed: stuck in a rut and going nowhere. They shrugged and headed back to the van. However, unlike the tractor, they quickly got their wheels into motion. Frank took the lead. "This is where the fun starts. Now you need to figure out how to sell these guys something they have absolutely no interest in! I'm sure you know how to do that!"

Larry answered confidently, "By finding some clever angles!"

"Well, Larry, my boy, it won't be easy but you can do it!"

"What's your read on the guy that set us up for failure?"

"From the looks of it, Ernie will be an interesting obstacle. He's an asshole! That's a given! The hardest thing to do in business, is to win over an asshole. Ninety-nine percent of the sales people out there shy away from that kind of challenge. Are you up to it?"

"Yes, sir!"

"If you're able to win over an asshole like Ernie, you'll put yourself into a very powerful position!"

"I love a challenge. Perhaps an 'end around' will be the play!"

"That a boy. That's the spirit. Okay, Larry, I'll let you go to work. Drop me off at my car. Looks like I might be able to catch an earlier flight to Denver. Lots of big stuff cooking in Denver!"

Daylight broke as Larry dropped off Frank. While the clouds of dust settled on the road behind Frank's car, Larry sat in his van, accessing and regrouping. Now what? He turned left and headed down the highway. Flier's Café would be the beginning of a revamped plan, perhaps the first step towards a clever angle. As he parked the van, he shook his head in affirmation.

Since the Flier's was only 2 miles from Town and Country's shop and the parking lot was full of pick-up trucks, it was worth a try.

A sign posted by the fire marshal stated that the Flier's capacity was limited to 40 occupants. There were easily 60 people squeezed into it. The smell of bacon sucked in customers from all corners of the county. Bingo! He spotted a man at the counter wearing a 'Town and Country' hat and sat next to him. Candy, the lone waitress, filled his coffee cup and took his order. In record time, she delivered pancakes surrounded by scrambled eggs and two crispy strips of bacon.

Larry thought to himself, "I'm glad she's not in the faucet business! She'd be a tough competitor!"

Candy worked the room like a politician seeking office. She squeezed between small spots of daylight, coffee pot in one hand and stacks of plates in the other. Her well-rounded body acted like the cushions of a bumper car. Smiling customers were sure to increase the size of their tips.

Larry started the conversation, "Candy is amazing!"

"You got that right!"

"So you work for Town and Country, huh?"

"Oh yeah, but don't tell anyone. I was supposed to be on the job, 'setting finish,' by now. If my boss knew I was running late, he'd kick my ass!"

"It doesn't sound like you're on Frank time!"

The puzzled plumber looked at Larry. "What?"

"Sorry, never mind."

The plumber was cramming the last few bites into his mouth. "Usually I'm here at 5:00, but the baby cried all night and I overslept!"

"I guess a baby can do that. Do lots of Town and Country guys eat here?"

"Shit yes. Even Red eats here. That's how you know it's good. Red eats breakfast here every day. He gets here when they open and is usually headed out the door about the time I get here. If the Flier's is good enough for Red, it's good enough for me!"

The plumber grabbed his check and was headed to the cash register before Larry stopped him. "What's your name?"

"Chip!"

"Well, Chip, it's great to meet you! Hand me that check; I'm buying you breakfast! Here's my card! I'm Larry with PROH$_2$O faucets."

"Wow, Larry, I guess it's my lucky day!"

Larry smiled at Chip and silently celebrated. As Chip squeezed past Candy to the door, Larry's booming voice pierced through the Flier's chaos: "Chip, the luck is all mine!"

CHAPTER 4

"Why is every day Wednesday?"

Mornings at The Ranch were rich with activity. Larry and Susan were in a race to the starting gate. Not just with each other, but against their biggest competitor of all: time. When the 5:30 AM buzzer rang, Susan immediately popped in a CD, usually the Beatles. Larry let Charlie out to ensure the perimeter of The Ranch was secure. The Ranch featured his and hers showers. By six they were out of the shower, frantic bodies scrambling through wardrobe closets. Their paths crossed in front of the vanity tops in the bathroom. A quick hug and kiss punctuated their love. As they separated, Larry yearned for a bit more, gently rubbing her back. The result of the loving embrace was a difficult read for Larry. A 'Susan Look' followed. Was it was a good look, or a bad one?

The result came swiftly! "Oh Larry, don't you know it's Wednesday? You know how busy Wednesdays are! I'll meet you in the kitchen! That's where you'll get your treat!"

"Really?"

"YES! It's pancake morning! I prepared the batter last night!"

It seemed to Larry that only Susan could make a pancake morning disappointing.

Back to the tasks at hand! The coffee was brewing and the cakes were griddling. Charlie eyed both Larry and Susan to make sure everything was okay. Little was said, but lots got done. Larry filled Charlie's food dish on the front porch and whined, "Why is every day Wednesday?"

Moments later Larry and Susan Schafer were both out the door, and into their cars, heading down Penny Lane, and into their own worlds.

The town of Lake Mathias was bordered by a rugged mountain range on the south and the lake itself to the north. Its eastern border stretched to March Air Force Base. On the other side of the base was Sunnymeade, the heart of the housing boom. Lumbering loads of trash heading west ten miles from the base would reach the regional refuse disposal site, the western boundary of Lake Mathias.

Precisely in the middle of those four points was downtown Lake Mathias. The majority of the 5,870 people lived within a six mile radius of downtown. The net result was a vast block of acreage untouched by bulldozers. The Lake Mathias housing moratorium put into effect August 1, 1983 mandated that homebuilders create new neighborhoods just about anywhere, but not there. Hence, homebuilders plowed their dollars into homes on the other side of the lake, south of the rugged mountain range, east of the air force base or west of the dump. Everywhere, except Lake Mathias!

The moratorium was slated to end July 31, 1987. The big question, in and around town, was centered on what the town council would do next: extend the moratorium or let builders dictate the town's future.

The revenue streams from the state and county flowed past Lake Mathias, not into it. Since wealthy and influential people did not live in the small town, no earmarks found their way there. Likewise, the town was not riddled with folks living below the poverty line. Residents were predominantly middle incomers living in the middle of nowhere.

There was one elementary school and one high school. They were the cultural centers of town. The mayor was a retired educator who was elected to the voluntary position unopposed. Mayor Sam Calhoun's most distinguishing qualities were his love for his '53 Chevy, his red suspenders, and his confident dedication to doing the right thing. The mayor was a popular topic at Sal's Cafe, the local diner.

The City Council members were elected, but also not paid. At one time there were seven, but in the last election there were only four names on the ballot, so those four became the council. In addition to Susan Schafer, the members consisted of Rex Fisher, a retired fireman; Blake Parker, a local realtor; and Jimmy Ray, a custom home builder. Since there was no city hall, weekly council meetings were held in the high school library on Wednesday afternoons. If a really hot topic was being discussed and the library was too small, the town hall meeting was moved to the high school auditorium. The final meeting that would determine the fate of the moratorium would definitely be in the auditorium.

Since it was Wednesday, Susan's day would include six periods of teaching English, a town council meeting, and perhaps a council wrap-up at Sal's. The '58 Corvette motored into the school parking lot. The air was filled with hope for the future, mating chess matches, and wide-eyed dreaming. Susan dressed professionally and conservatively. Black pants and white blouse buttoned snugly to the neck. Her hair was tightly knotted in a bun. No flashy jewelry. No make-up. Mrs. Schafer was all business and no nonsense. Her politics were liberal, but when she walked through the gates of the school, discipline was the rule. Students both feared and respected her. She was strict and a brutally tough grader. Some semesters no students earned an 'A' in her class.

The bell rang. Students, excited about the school year's end in two days, Friday the 26th of June, scrambled for their seats. It was first period and Mrs. Schafer was at the helm of a ship whose crew questioned nothing.

"Good morning, class. Today we are discussing the poetry of John Lennon. This material is not in your English literature textbook. I'm passing out supplemental materials for this discussion. Please read the lyrical poem, 'Imagine', to yourself three times."

Mrs. Shafer's classroom was now as quiet as a Lake Mathias night. Once the eyes of her students were all focused back at her, the teacher continued, "Cleverly and creatively crafted poetry can paint pictures in the mind, raise the spirit of the soul, and kindle fires in the heart. The author plays a 'what if' game that challenges us to 'imagine' a united, harmonious world. Philosophical questions ask us to ponder what the world would be like if there were no religion, countries, or conflicts among the world's people. I know most of you have probably heard this song, but have you really focused on the lyrics?" There were a couple of 'yes' headshakes, but the rest of the class shook their heads 'no'. "Tell me what the words mean to you and how you feel about them. Any volunteers?"

Peter was the first to respond, "It's like a perfect world where everybody is happy and there's no hatred, just love."

Mary spoke up next, "I want to live there. I love the peace and harmony. But, there's no America?"

Charles chipped in, "How can I possibly imagine the whole world getting along, when I don't even get along with my brother?"

Paul took a turn, "In this utopia, what if there are bad people? What do we do with them? What if I'm doing all the work, and my neighbor is lazy?"

Amelia spoke up, "I pray to God every day of my life. Will that be forbidden? Will I go to hell? Will everybody go to hell? If there is no heaven and no hell, where will we go?"

Mrs. Schafer challenged creative thought by adding an open-ended overview, "Poetry and literature are open to the interpretation of the reader. That is why scholars of all ages for many centuries have debated the contents and meaning of the written word so vigorously. Since only the author knows his or her real message and intent, there are really no right or wrong interpretations.

"Many people believe John Lennon's message was that it's healthy to dream of beautiful things, even if they seem illogical, or improbable. If there was ever to be world peace and harmony, we would need to dream it and work towards its achievement. If the people of the world continue their vicious hatred and reckless bloodshed, no one on earth will survive to write the story. The ultimate irony, of course, was that John Lennon was shot and killed in the world he tried to warn us about. Other people might interpret the poem as an argument for socialism. What do you think? Let's explore your interpretation. Your assignment for tomorrow is to write an essay that expresses how you feel about the message of the poem."

Suzie raised her hand. "How long should the essay be?"

Susan responded quickly, "From one word to a thousand. Any other questions?"

The room was quiet. The teacher wasn't sure if the silence of the students was due to a light turning on in their heads, or the silence of lost souls looking for the light. The following five periods of classes journeyed through the material in similar fashion.

The final bell of the day rang on cue. Susan Schafer stuffed stacks of papers and books into her shoulder bag. It was time to switch gears to community service, so off to the library she went. As she weaved and bobbed down the hallway, she lamented that she really preferred kids over adults. As for the adults, she was conflicted. Who was easier to reason with, Larry or her fellow council members? That was a toss-up, at best.

Susan entered the library. Rex, wearing shorts, golf shirt, and tennis shoes, was already there. He was a retired fireman with a staunch union loyalty. In crucial votes, Susan and Rex were usually on the same page, but still, Susan kept Rex at arm's length. There was just something about him that caused her to question his motives.

As for Blake and Jimmy, they were typically on the other side of the debates. Label them capitalistic entrepreneurs. Because she was married to Larry, Susan had lots of experience with this variety of trench warfare. Mayor Sam was a balanced moderate and skilled swing man.

Blake, the realtor, walked in: slick hair, pressed white shirt, and tie. Then custom homebuilder, Jimmy: wearing Levis, pocket tee shirt, and work boots. Last to arrive, as usual, Mayor Sam: always cool and calm, never hurried. The mayor wore his trademark red suspenders that stretched over his proud belly.

Citizens were invited to attend some council meetings, but that was not the case on this day. Today's meeting would be informal, but would set groundwork for the main event. Should the moratorium be allowed to expire or should it be extended; if so, for how long and under what conditions?

Seated alone, taking the minutes of the meeting was, Kathleen, the school secretary. An arrangement with the school district made this possible. Mayor Sam, as always, made his opening remarks and then set the agenda. "Dedicated members of the town council of Lake Mathias, thank you for serving this wonderful community. To begin with, I will remind you of the town charter which calls for the mayor to vote only if needed for a tie-breaker."

Sam started every meeting with this exact text. Like a three course meal, these opening remarks were the appetizer; then, the main course, which on this day, was the disposition of the moratorium.

"We have a once in a lifetime opportunity to set the direction for this town's future. Whatever our decision, it will be liked by some and hated by many. If history determines that we made the wrong decision, we will be blamed. If we make the right decision, no one will ever acknowledge that we set the right course. Fortunately the town pays us big money to make this decision!"

As the council burst into hearty laughter, Mayor Sam continued, "By my calendar, after today, we have two more exasperating meetings in July to look at this thing top to bottom, inside and out. As you know, the library is not available next Wednesday, July 1st because it will be processing text books. Because of a conflict with the Independence week fundraising bake sale, we're not meeting Wednesday July 8th. And, the library will not be available on the 15th because of a book fare.

"That brings us to the 22nd. Please have your due-diligence completed so we can really get down to business right here in the library on July 22nd. The meeting at 5 PM on the 29th will be town hall style in the auditorium. The eyes of our neighbors will be upon us like magnifiers burning holes in our hearts. Given the critical nature, I suggest we table all other issues until August. All in favor say, 'Aye.'"

The vote was unanimous.

"Now, let's get the ball rolling. The agenda for today will be short and sweet. Everybody will give their point of view, the fewer words the better. Then we're going to go over to Sal's to hash this thing out a bit. All in favor say 'Aye.'"

Again, a unanimous vote.

Jimmy, who was never shy, said, "Well, the town's dying. If we don't give it a heart transplant, it'll be dead before you know it!"

Rex was next, saying, "I see it both ways. A small town is great, but it's really hard to stay in time with the world if the battery on your watch is dead. It might be smart to open this thing up and see what happens."

Blake stepped right up. "Why in the hell would people want to stay here if they're going broke. Property values here are thirty percent less than those in neighboring towns. Builders building new communities would make people take notice of this town. When that happens, property values will soar and businesses like Sal's will be standing room only. People commuting to jobs today might find good jobs in town tomorrow. As for quality of life, builders would put in parks and community centers. This town would attract lots of people looking for a better life."

Sam stepped in, "Damn, Blake, I said a few words, not a narrative from 'Gone with the Wind'. Okay, Susan, got any ideas?"

"Personally, I like the feel of a small sleepy town. I think we can all agree that we were drawn to this town because it's small and sleepy. Larry and I came here because we could get acreage and privacy for the same price as a tract home in the bigger cities. But, still, I just don't know. Sometimes the things that have been are not in the best interest of what is yet to be. On the other hand, if you believe that dropping the moratorium will inspire business people to improve the quality of life, you must believe in Santa Claus. Builders might build houses, but they'll only spend money on a community, like ours, if it benefits them."

Sam commented as he got up from his chair, "Susan, if I wasn't confused before, I am now. Well, folks, I need to digest those comments a bit. Let's head over to Sal's!"

Susan stopped him in his tracks, "Sam, surely you have a comment on this critical topic!"

"We should make a decision that is best for the people of the town. I'll meet you at Sal's!"

Sal's Diner was the place to drink a tall glass of ice cold lemonade on a hot summer day. Seated together on the patio at their traditional round table, the council members randomly shared pro and con arguments. Sal made it a point to hear words not directed at him and, in passing, quick to throw in his viewpoint. In this session, there were many smart comments made by all the council members. Some were even brilliant. But the comment that the mayor made was the one that would have the biggest impact. "Money will influence the moratorium and the direction of the town. There will be money out there to influence your vote, and lots of it. So be careful about what you think and do. Be careful who you talk to. And whatever side you may be leaning, ask yourself if it will benefit the people of the town or outsiders who want to capitalize on what we've got. Anything that falls short of doing the right thing is unacceptable."

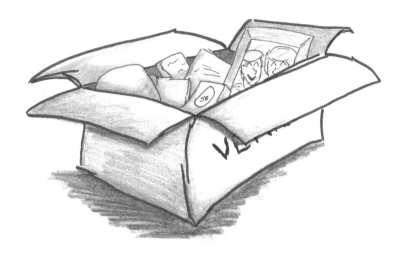

CHAPTER 5

"The Box"

Charlie was the 'Master of the Ranch'. Susan was the queen of the house. And Larry? He was the king of the garage. On this Saturday, Larry would re-connect with the kingdom he had been neglecting. The game plan was to sort, organize and toss. The Astro's seats had already been removed, so it was now a cargo van. With Charlie by his side, Larry balanced his coffee while slowly rolling up the garage door. Charlie was filled with excitement and anticipation because he knew that by afternoon he and Larry would be on a road trip to the dump.

The easy part of the process was thinning out $PROH_2O$ samples, literature, and displays. There was easily a cargo load of work material in the garage collection, and two thirds of it would end up in the Astro and head to the dump. That left a third of the van for household discards that Susan had moved to the garage. Larry's philosophy was, "When in doubt, throw it out!"

The van was full, Larry's coffee cup was empty, and Charlie sensed their reward: a trip to the dump. A final box was left to dispatch or keep. There were two faded markings on the carton. One said 'keep', the other said 'Ventura'. Larry opened the mystery box and stared at the contents. "Wow, Charlie, I had no idea this stuff was still around!"

Wild thoughts flew around Larry's mind like a racquetball careening inside his square head. "Since she kept this box around all this time, why is she throwing it away now?"

Charlie looked as befuddled as Larry. "What was the hold-up?"

"Look, here's a picture of me and Susan at Disneyland….and here's a Ventura College handbook. And these, these are my business cards from Dick's Plumbing. That's where I met Frank! Wow!"

Charlie responded with a rare whiney bark. Larry proceeded to dig through the contents, then stopped and stared. He could not believe the next treasure. "Here's a collector's item, an ancient menu from Johnny's Beach Bungalow!"

Susan was not home; she was out shopping in Riverside. "I can't believe she put this box of history out here in the garage without telling me. Look here, our Disneyland ticket stubs!"

In 1972, Larry Schafer and Susan Fleming met, fell in love, and were married. They made their nest, in a midtown 1927 Ventura bungalow, on San Nicholas Street.

"Charlie, I remember it like it was yesterday…"

For most of the students at Ventura College, it was a day that in future years would be easily forgotten. But for Larry and Susan, it was a day they would always remember. The day that two crazy kids tripped, fell, and recovered. Their comeback was only matched by Charlie, who was about to meet his fate when Larry and Susan rescued him from the pound.

It was the first day of the spring semester. Larry took his seat in Business 101 wearing the same thing he wore every single day: Levis crowned with a white tee shirt, socks, and sneakers. On cold foggy mornings, a blue sweatshirt was pulled over his curly head. He was determining his career path through the process of elimination. If the subject did not suit him, careers associated with those classes were crossed off his list. The instructor walked into a standing room only classroom. She spoke slowly, clearly, and loudly.

"Ladies and Gentlemen, you have chosen to enroll in my Business 101 class. Since this IS a business class, the course will be conducted in a business-like manner. If it is your intention to stay enrolled, you must, beginning with the next scheduled class, adhere to the following business dress code: Ladies must wear skirts cut below the knee, a long sleeve blouse, nylons and heels. As for the gentlemen: pressed slacks, long-sleeved shirt, tie, and dress shoes. If these rules do not suit you, step to the back of the room to pick up a class withdrawal card!"

Larry was never too shy to ask a question, "Professor, is there any flexibility in those rules? I work in a plumbing shop between classes. I can't dress like that when I'm threading pipe!"

"The rules that I outlined do have flexibility. You may wear any color tie that you wish!"

During the stampede to pick-up withdrawal cards, Larry mentally crossed off his list any career that had to do with business. There were two stacks of withdrawal cards on the table. As Larry grabbed his card and turned to his left to exit, a cute brunette wearing a mini skirt and boots turned to her right to exit. The result was a head-on collision that featured flying bags, books, and body parts. If that collision was between cars, ambulances and tow trucks would have been mobilized. As the two fallen strangers picked themselves up, Larry gathered himself. "Hi, my name's Larry. I think we both agree that we're not going into business!"

Susan was too agitated to smile, but managed an aggravated sigh. "Is this how you meet girls?"

Larry shrugged. "This is a test. What do you think?"

"I think that I never want to see you again!"

"So a kiss is out of the question?"

"What did you say your name is again?"

"Larry!"

"Okay, Larry, I can see you're pretty smooth with the one-liners!"

"I'm sorry, I don't think I caught your name."

Larry was now on the receiving end of piercing brown eyes and a smirking voice, "What is it with you? My name is Susan!"

"Hi, Suzie!"

"On top of your other bad qualities, your hearing is bad! I said Susan, not Suzie! Do not call me Suzie! Get it?"

"Sorry, Susan. My name is Laurenz, but people call me Larry, so I just figured..."

"If you don't think too good, don't think too much!"

Larry was undeterred. "I would love to buy you a cup of coffee."

That was the first time Larry saw the 'Susan Look' in play, a look that would be as familiar as a good night kiss. Her head was tilted stiffly forward, her eyes were frozen. Her mouth was puckered. "If I say yes, will you promise me that you will stay out of my life forever?"

"Can I answer that after we have coffee?"

Piercing brown eyes transformed into rolling brown tumblers. Was there a well-disguised hint of a smile in that alluring face? There seemed to be opposing magnetic forces in play: delicious sweetness and competitive fire. The conversation with Susan rekindled the spirit that Larry felt when he was on the high school debate team. This girl named Susan was giving Larry a run for his money.

"Are you always this difficult?"

"Susan, you're throwing lots of questions at me. I really don't want to screw up the answers. I think a lot better when I'm sipping coffee. How about it?"

"Okay, I have forty minutes before my next class, but I intend to keep a suspicious eye on you! There is something about you that is not quite normal!"

Now seated and relaxed, the iceberg between the strangers started to melt. Each sip of coffee was followed by friendly bantering, smiles, and laughter. Larry loved her shapely shapes. Her hypnotic brown eyes mesmerized him. As she spoke, he was falling in love with her sharp, blunt tongue. He had been with sappy girls. They bored him. Susan was different; she was a mysterious combination of smart, confident, and beautiful. Susan would be a challenge. That was a given! But, she would be worth it!

Susan laughed, and she laughed, and she laughed. Larry made her laugh. Laughter made her tingle inside. She hated the dating game. Boring men fumbling for words to gain her affection revolted her. Larry seemed different, certainly not normal, but different in a fun way. Larry was good medicine.

"Alright, Larry, it's just about time for class. I have a test for you."

"A test?"

"Question number one: Are you always this difficult?"

"Absolutely!"

"You're lucky that I prefer difficult men. Question number two! Now that we've had coffee, do you promise to stay out of my life forever?"

"Absolutely not!"

"Good work, Larry. I'll give you a 'B'!"

Larry stared at her big brown eyes. "I thought surely I would get an 'A'!"

"You're very lucky to get a 'B'. I am NOT an easy grader!"

"What does it take to get an 'A' in your class?"

"If you're really lucky, you might find out some day. So, where are you taking me on our first date?"

"Disneyland!"

"Perfect, I love Disneyland. Here's my phone number. Call me with the details!"

Susan planted a kiss on Larry's beet red cheek, turned, and sauntered away.

Charlie barked sharply to awaken Larry from his daydream. This daydream might be a case study for psychologists. "Charlie, the first 55 minutes of my life with Susan exhausted me. I was a wet noodle in her bowl of soup!"

Charlie plopped down and rested his head on his paws. It was becoming apparent that the trip to the dump was being delayed by a cardboard box.

The daydream continued...

It was Saturday; oh so many Saturdays ago. The hook was set. Larry and Susan were going to Disneyland. Larry would pick up Susan at 2:30. He worked his way through college with minimum wage paychecks from Dick's Plumbing. Since the shop was open until 1 PM on Saturdays, he would barely have time to quickly shower and pick her up.

Larry was Dick's only employee. His job consisted of doing anything that Steve, the owner, did not want to do: sweeping the floors, cleaning the bathroom, and unloading trucks. When Steve was out of the shop, Larry got to do what he loved best: selling plumbing products to customers clutching old rusted parts that needed to be replaced. He became an expert in the world of faucets, toilets, and pipe. Most of the customers were regulars who knew and liked Larry.

At about noon, Big Ben, Dick's best customer came in with a long list of galvanized pipe to cut and thread to size. This involved operating a pipe cutting and threading machine. Since the machine squirted oil into its dyes, there was no way to do this job without smelling like oil. The timing could not have been worse! It was his first date with Susan and he would smell like pipe cutting oil. His record of lousy first impressions would continue.

Big Ben was a giant of a man with a smile to match. When customers needed an expert to fix their tired plumbing, Larry always recommended Big Ben. Big Ben was a real life version of 'Big John', from the famous song about a miner who stood six foot five and weighed 245. Ben came over to check on the progress. It was 12:58 and Larry was just about finished, but certainly not happy. Big Ben's giant hands slapped Larry gently on his slouched shoulders. His round face was tough but compassionate. "What's got you frazzled?"

"I have a big date and I'm going to smell like oil!"

"Sorry about that. You should have said something. I could have cut and threaded the pipe myself!"

"Not your fault, Ben."

"Pay attention, Larry!"

"To what?"

"You are one very lucky guy!"

"How do you figure that?"

"You're earning enough to get yourself through school, right?"

"Well, yeah."

"And you're learning about plumbing, something that will help you the rest of your life!"

A frustrated Larry turned to Ben and replied, "Let me assure you, when I finish college I will never, ever have anything to do with plumbing!"

Ben shook his head and smiled as the men loaded the custom load of freshly threaded pipe onto his truck.

By 1:10 Larry was out the door and off to shower. At 2:30 sharp, Susan, cute as a VW love bug, was seated next to him in his 1961 Volkswagen Beetle.

Susan sniffed her nose to identify a strange scent. "What's that smell?"

Larry answered as he shifted the 1200cc bug into fourth gear. "That's cutting oil. Isn't it great?"

"Not really."

As Larry described his pipe cutting morning with Big Ben, Susan smiled and shook her head. She had never before met anyone like this quirky guy named Larry Schafer.

Larry figured that they would arrive at Disneyland at about 4:30. As they proceeded up the Conejo Grade, a climbing stretch of highway that bridged cool sea air to warm dry air, Larry down-shifted into third gear. That made the motor sound like a blender in turbo speed. Susan was accustomed to muscle cars. The VW was a wimpy car. Cute, but wimpy. At the top of the grade the bug regained its maximum speed of 65. Even then, they were struggling to keep up with the speed of traffic, even in the slow lane.

"Larry, trucks are passing us!"

"Yeah, I'm used to it. But up ahead there is a nice downhill run. She'll do 72 down hills!"

Before they hit the down-hill stretch, the bug sputtered to a stop along the side of the highway. "Don't panic, Susan, I can fix it. It's those damn points. Sometimes they just shut down on me!"

Susan had no clue what Larry was talking about. It had just become apparent to her that the motor was in the rear and not the front. But, Susan was a doer, not a watcher. Larry had the hood propped open. Susan leaned forward as a breeze teased up her mini skirt. Cars speeding by honked. "I'm pretty handy! Maybe I can help!"

"Not really, it's a one man job. This happens every three to four weeks. Sorry about the poor timing. Maybe you should get back in the car before you cause an accident."

Larry kept the tools to re-set the engine's points in the front trunk of his bug. It was just a matter of prying open the distributor cap, rotating the cam to the maximum point and then resetting the gap of the points to .16 mm. Larry had done this so frequently that he could eyeball .16 mm. "Okay, we're all set!"

Susan smiled at Larry again. "I think I'm getting the full treatment. Are you this smooth with all the girls you date?"

"Well, I've done a little bit of dating, but for some unknown reason, I'm just not a lady's man. I can't understand it, can you?"

"Beats the heck out of me, Larry, I am absolutely dumbfounded!"

Meanwhile back at The Ranch...

"Charlie, wake up, it's time to go to the dump!"

Larry put the box of history in a safe spot in the garage. After Charlie jumped into the back seat, Larry slid behind the wheel and down the road they went.

Charlie's tail communicated his excitement. He loved a road trip. And there was no better road trip than a ride with Larry in the Astro to the dump. The last three miles were Charlie's favorite part. That stretch featured a tight zigzag pattern, which meant the Astro would be traveling about 15 MPH, the ideal speed for Charlie to stick his big head out of the window to taste, feel, and smell the essence of the dump.

The unique combination of the mildewed, rancid, and decaying rubbish created the smell of a delicious witch's stew. Charlie's nostrils eagerly inhaled the concoction. His ears filtered the sounds of trash trucks dumping their loads. This, thought Charlie, will be a wonderful day after all!

Larry took a breath; the pungent smell overwhelming his senses. "Man oh man, it stinks here!"

Charlie knew that Larry didn't appreciate good sniffing. He wondered why God even provided humans with noses. They certainly did not appreciate the wonder of life's invigorating aromas.

As Charlie squirmed to fit more of his head out the window, Larry's mind wandered back to Disneyland...

It was a long walk from the parking lot to the Disneyland ticket cashier. But Larry loved every step. Susan was wearing a bright red mini-skirt. Her legs stretched longer than long and were delightfully shaped. Even stems that led bees to a flower in full bloom were not this scrumptious. As they walked, Susan grabbed his hand. He was thankful that she was not reluctant to hold an oil-stinky hand.

Larry stepped up to the ticket window. "Two tickets, please!"

Susan jumped in. "Make that one!"

Now Larry was really confused.

"I pay my own way. I refuse to owe you or anyone else anything! You and I are just becoming friends. At this point, it's hard to tell where we're headed, if anywhere at all. The one thing I'm sure of, is that I am NOT a purchased commodity!"

Larry really didn't understand girls. And this girl, of all girls, continued to make him scratch his square head. As they dined at 'The Pirates of the Caribbean', the young couple laughed, laughed, and laughed. Larry fidgeted when he was with girls. But, it was different with Susan. He actually felt relaxed. The bill came. At Susan's insistence, they split it right down the middle.

As they headed to the 'Rocket Jet' ride, grumbling clouds dropped a drizzle. By the time they were tandemly positioned, buckets of rain started pouring. As the rocket rollercoaster spun around, Susan snuggled back against Larry's chest and turned to look at him. Larry was no expert, but he was pretty sure that she wanted him to kiss her. As their eyes and lips met, a Beatles tune, 'All you Need is Love', serenaded the young lovers in the rain.

As they left the 'Rockets' sopping and drenched, they clutched hands and headed for the car. The downpour shortened their day at Disneyland, but Cupid had shot an arrow through their hearts. As their rain soaked bodies returned to the VW, the young couple secretly acknowledged that their romance was growing like a spring flower after a spring drizzle.

On the ride home, Larry was floor-boarding the VW to its maximum speed of 72 MPH. They were almost to Ventura when the car started to sputter and stammer, again.

"Let me guess, it's the points!"

Larry reached over and flipped a lever beneath the dash. "Good guess, but it's just the gas!"

"Are we on empty?"

"No, we now have 1.5 gallons in the tank! The reserve fuel tap lever I just flipped activated the additional gas!"

Susan looked at the dash. "No wonder you were sputtering. You have no fuel gauge!"

"That's why they put in the reserve fuel tap."

"I think I prefer American cars over foreign cars. We wouldn't have any of these issues if we were riding in a Corvette!"

Larry's brain leaped back to the present…

The Astro came to a halt. Larry and Charlie got out. Charlie loved every second of the experience. In the first five minutes, he lifted his leg on seventeen spots. Only 'The Master of the Ranch' could find a Jelly Bean in Life at the dump.

After Larry dragged the trash out of the van, he and Charlie hit the road. As they traveled the dusty road home, Larry's mind returned to Ventura…

"Susan, have you ever seen the grunion run?"

"What's that?"

"At high tide, the ocean washes up boat loads of shiny silver fish that dig holes in the sand for spawning. The grunions are running tonight!"

Larry and Susan's bare toes were happy in the silky sand. The waves pounded a peaceful rhythm. They never saw any silver grunion, but it was understandable. In the game of life, shiny silver fish are trumped by hearts on fire.

The grand finale of the day was dinner at Johnny's Beach Bungalow, a local favorite located at the end of Seaward Avenue and just steps from the beach. Since Johnny's was overflowing with jolly patrons, merely squeezing through the entrance was a challenge. The bar was packed and the liquor was flowing. In the dining room, there were twelve tables squeezed into a six table space. The patrons were all laughing. It may not have been the 'happiest place on earth', but it was darn close.

After cramming two chairs around a small table, the young lovers were comfortably sipping on root beers. Susan looked outside and watched a Signet Red 1958 Corvette park in front of the restaurant. "Larry, look at THAT car! That's what we should be riding in!"

The owner of the Corvette grabbed the guitar that was in his back seat. He entered the restaurant and stood in the doorway. Johnny, the owner of Johnny's Beach Bungalow, squeezed through the crowd to greet his guest. The patrons who recognized the musician started applauding like fans celebrating a touchdown at a football game!

Larry recalled how exhilarating it felt to overcome the unrelenting stench of oil stinky hands and end his long string of horrible 'first dates'. That streak started in high school, when he was so mesmerized by 'Sweet Pea Pam', that he neglected job one, minding the steering wheel. The tragic end to that first date was that his car jumped the curb in front of her house and finally came to rest on her front lawn. Needless to say, there was never a second date.

Larry celebrated the musician and the death of the agonizing chain of bad first dates like a kid riding his bike for the first time without training wheels. Susan jumped up and down as if she had just won a million dollar jackpot in Las Vegas.

Johnny and his friend with the guitar squeezed their way to the grand piano. Johnny climbed onto the bench and shouted, "Friends, may I have your attention, please! I have an important announcement. It is very likely that tonight's surprise will be remembered forevermore. My friend, John Lennon, has generously offered to play his favorite songs for you tonight!"

Seated atop the grand piano with his Yamaha acoustical guitar, John Lennon's songs filled the restaurant for nearly an hour. An angel with a harp would have played second fiddle to this heavenly performance. The crowd of sixty-four screaming worshippers flew 'across the universe' with John Lennon that night. For the finale, he was seated at the piano to sing his legendary song, 'Imagine'. At the conclusion of the concert that Larry and Susan would later refer to as the 'Imagine Concert', The Beach Bungalow faithful erupted in a glorious celebration of applause. The Beatles legend then bowed three times and slowly made his way to his dining table in the corner of the restaurant. This route put Larry and Susan directly in his path.

Larry wasn't sure why John Lennon chose to stop in front of their table. Was it Susan's smile or her red miniskirt, shrunk from the wetness? In any event, John Lennon was stopped in his tracks. As be bowed his head, he eloquently picked up her hand and kissed it.

For the very first time in her life, Susan Fleming was speechless!

CHAPTER 6

"Ping Pong"

Larry, Susan, and Charlie weaved their way down a ranch trail made from broken chunks of concrete buried in the earth with the smooth side up. The trail was both interesting and 'ranchy'. Those were the criteria for the Schafers' ranch projects. The labor pool for projects consisted of Larry, Susan, and their friend Joe, a hired helper. As they progressed down the trail, the threesome was startled to see a Chaparral Yucca plant that had pushed a giant stalk twelve feet towards the sky out of its spiny base.

Susan was astounded. "That's as remarkable as the bean sprout that Jack climbed in the fairy tale! I was out here a few days ago, and there was nothing!"

Every time a yucca at 'The Ranch' raised a stalk, the event was as magnificent as a falling star on a dark moonless night. The dense stalk was the diameter of a ranch cucumber and seemingly grew overnight.

Petals of white flowers sprouted from the upper portion of the column. Charlie raised his leg to christen a new member of the family. He evidently believed that 'The Ranch' was home to so many yuccas because of his ritual of christening the shooting stalks by raising his leg on the base.

In reality, a small moth is the secret to the yucca's survival and proliferation. Remarkably, nature genetically programmed the 'yucca moth' to stuff a ball of pollen into the stigma of the flower. Were it not for that moth, yucca plants would not reproduce, and the world would possess one less miracle.

Once they reached the garden, the Schafers filled a bag with fresh ranch vegetables that would be the heart of their dinner. Two squash, two tomatoes, and an onion would do the trick.

As they circled back, Larry headed to the BBQ and Susan to the kitchen. There was a cavernous divide between Larry and Susan when they argued, but projects that required no verbal communication were completed as if the Schafers were well-oiled gears with the ability to turn the earth on its axis.

As Larry fired up the BBQ, he marveled at the splendor and tranquility of a ranch day as it nears its end. Susan brought out two filet mignons and a basket of zucchini and onions. By the time the steaks and zucchini were cooked to perfection, Susan had prepared a tomato salad and uncorked a bottle of wine. Charlie worked his way back and forth between Larry and Susan to ensure everything was okay. After the Schafers took their seats, Charlie plopped down in a neutral corner between them.

They sat on the front deck, a quiet corner of the universe known by many in the plant and animal community but only a sprinkling of humans. The road in front of 'The Ranch' was dirt. There were no street lights and there was very little coming or going. Nature's celebration occasionally broke the stark sound of ranch silence. The wise owl began making its loops and hooting his hoots as the sun moved slowly towards the Pacific Ocean.

"Susan, tomorrow will be a really big day!"

"Are you putting together plans to overthrow the government and lead the free world? Pass me the salt, please."

"Oh no, I'm remaining on the sidelines in the political arena, but I've planned a strategic business move. Tomorrow is the first day of implementation! These steaks are sure tasty. How was school today?"

"You know what, Larry, I know there are problems out there, but I think this next generation will be up for the challenge!"

Larry reached for the bottle of merlot. "That's exactly why we should have children. I'm positive we'd raise the kind of kids that were part of the solution and not part of the problem! We should have children so there will be reinforcements for the kids fixing the craziness. Would you like some more wine?"

"I'll give you a yes on wine and a no on children!"

"Why won't you have children with me?"

"I have children! They are in my English class. And then, I come home and babysit the biggest kid I know!"

"You shouldn't be so hard on Charlie!"

Larry was now on the receiving end of a 'Susan look'.

Dinner at The Ranch was a special time for Larry, Susan and, of course, Charlie. Charlie loved Larry and Susan equally and took no sides, but at times used body language to guide and encourage family harmony.

Conversations were verbal ping pong matches. A slam to the corner of the table was always just one play away. Fifteen years earlier, on San Nicholas Street, real ping pong was played in the living room. Now the game had moved to the kitchen without a table, paddles, or balls.

"I'll tell you what Susan: thank goodness Ronald Reagan is president. I don't trust those Russian communists one bit! And our president is not afraid to stand up to them!"

"So the game of Star Wars he is playing: Is that real leadership or is he inviting World War III?"

"Even you must acknowledge that Reagan's demand last month for the Berlin Wall to be taken down was both courageous and Kennedy-'esque'!"

"So now you're comparing Reagan to Kennedy?"

"This tomato salad is absolutely delicious. Mark my words, it will be written in textbooks for future generations to read, that Ronald Reagan compares favorably with George Washington, Abraham Lincoln and yes, even, your beloved John F. Kennedy!"

"Those jelly beans are causing you to hallucinate! You better back off of them!"

Larry just smiled. Susan shook her head. Charlie sensed that left-overs would be headed his way.

As they cleared the table, Susan circled back. "So Mr. Faucet-business-man, what is this grand plan you are implementing?"

"Charlie and I will be on a job site road trip to determine how $PROH_2O$ faucets will solve problems that Town and Country Plumbing has no idea they have."

"How will you discover problems that they know nothing of?"

"That's what I call professional salesmanship!"

"By the way, Larry, I'm missing a box."

"What?"

"For years, I've planned to make a scrap-book that held the history of you and me. Since summer vacation is at my doorstep, I dug the box up from underneath the bed."

"Hold that thought."

Larry headed out to the garage and returned with the box of nostalgia. "Here you go!"

Susan lowered her chin and gave Larry another look. "How did you end up with my special box? And why did you not tell me you had it?"

"Well, since you put it in the garage, I assumed you were throwing it out. You have never, ever put anything you want to keep in the garage. You're darn lucky that box, which evidently you wanted to keep, didn't end up at the dump!"

"Since the contents of my scrapbook are contained in that box, why would I throw it away?"

"Exactly! That's exactly what I was wondering! Since you kept that box all of these years, why would you throw it away now?"

Susan was exhausted. "I've got nothing more to say about this! I'm done! Thank you for not discarding the box that I've been saving for fifteen years; a box you were not supposed to have in the first place!"

Larry looked at Susan. Charlie looked at Larry and located a neutral corner. The box that had delayed his trip to the dump had created a ranch full of turmoil. Shots were expertly handled, back and forth in the Schafers' verbal ping pong game; each play was strategic. The goal was to set up the un-returnable slam to the corner. Charlie sensed trouble, but also smelled food that might be heading his way. Larry scratched his head and filled Charlie's bowl with zucchini and trimmed steak. "So what's up with the moratorium in town?"

"You should attend the meeting and find out! This is a very important issue! I'm sure the business people you talk to all want the moratorium to die!"

Larry looked directly into Susan's sizzling eyes. "Lots of people think that this town could actually become special if government didn't strangle it!"

"The will of the people will determine if Lake Mathias will remain a small peaceful town or turn into another city that attracts the wrong people and chases out the right people!"

"So let me guess, the wrong people are business people?"

"That's not what I said, but I like living in a small town, and I thought you did too!"

Charlie wished it was bedtime.

Larry wiped the counter as Susan loaded the last dinner plate into the dishwasher.

"I would love to take you out into the real world I live in for a day. Maybe, just maybe, you would find that business people are really not the enemy!"

Susan rolled her eyes. "When we dropped out of Business 101 at Ventura College, we both vowed to stay clear of big business. I kept my end of the bargain! What happened to you?"

"I guess I went down the same path as our president. Ronald Reagan was a Democrat until he finally figured out what life was like in the real world. A big part of the real world is capitalism. Independently thinking people in my world, love this country, love free enterprise, and hate the government sticking its nose where it doesn't belong!"

"So that's why there are gas lines and ridiculous gas prices that people can't afford? The government isn't sticking it to the people. It's the oil companies!"

"Jimmy Carter, a Democrat, was president in 1979 when we had gas lines!"

"The problem in this country is that no president has been able to control big business!"

"Free enterprise is not perfect, but it's the best thing out there. Do you know what the president said are the nine most dangerous words in the English language?"

"I can hardly wait to hear the answer to this one!"

Larry took a deep breath. Charlie shook his head as if to warn Larry not to repeat the nine words. But Larry was on a mission. He was going for the slam to the corner. "Ronald Reagan said the nine most dangerous words in the English language are, 'I'm with the government. I'm here to help you!'"

"You need to stop eating jelly beans! Evidently they squelch logical thinking! Look what they've done to the president!"

Point-game-match!

Charlie got his wish. A late dinner and Larry-Susan verbal ping pong moved the clock to the Schafers' bedtime. Down the hall moved the procession, Susan followed by Larry and then Charlie. Larry and Susan worked their way through the tail end of their daily routine culminating with a quick kiss and reciprocal love pats.

Charlie had seen enough. His eyes were locked down. His tail had retreated. He whined as if to say that his masters needed to replace their verbal ping pong with a real table, real paddles, and real balls. Charlie was a wonderful example of how much peace can exist on earth when words don't get in the way. He didn't understand why his favorite treat, jelly beans, had fueled such a bitter ping pong match.

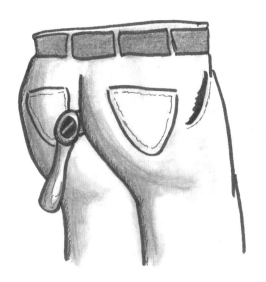

CHAPTER 7

"Ratchet-Ass"

It was a BIG day: the day Larry and Charlie would take a road trip to the Flier's together. Larry, without the aid of an alarm clock, sneaked out of bed on the tips of his clumsy toes. To make sure he did not awaken Susan, he showered in the bath down the hall. Since it was a jobsite day, slacks and sports coat were not in play. It was a Levis and tennis shoes day. Larry was more round than chiseled, so his jeans fit loosely around his thirty-eight inch waistline. His six foot two inch frame comfortably carried his weight. He was built more for power than finesse. His duck-like shuffling feet barely left the ground. The goal was to get both him and Charlie out the door by 4 AM, without waking up Susan.

Larry's schedule had him arriving to the Flier's Café at 4:15 on Frank time. As he settled into his Astro seat, Charlie's tail gyrated like a windshield wiper on hyper speed. Larry turned his wrist to check the time on his watch, but much to his dismay, he wasn't wearing it! A trip back into the house to find his watch was now in play.

After he located his house key he headed back to the house while Charlie faithfully waited in the van. Larry headed down the hallway, and made his way to the bedroom. Since he always left his watch on the dresser, he reached on top of it, but found nothing. Susan was still asleep. That was good, but Larry couldn't find his watch. That was bad. It would be impossible for him to keep his day on schedule without his watch. Larry's days, weeks and months revolved around keeping a regimented schedule. Without a watch, he was screwed. His brain was scrambling for a logical answer.

He mumbled secret words in his head as he shook it in frustration, "I know! It must have fallen from the dresser to the floor!"

Larry turned on the hall light, hoping it would not awaken Susan. He crawled around the floor like Charlie sniffing for a bone. Nothing! He started shuffling back to the hall ever so quietly, when Susan sat up, rubbed her sleepy eyes, and solved the mystery. "Larry! Your watch is on the bathroom counter. After I stepped on it, I picked it up and got it out of harm's way!"

"Thank you, Susan!"

Larry was not sure how Susan, in a deep sleep, knew what he was looking for, but he was grateful.

"You and Charlie need to be careful. I'm not sure I like the idea of you two at a construction site!"

"We'll be okay. See ya!"

In spite of the late start, Larry and Charlie arrived at the Flier's at 4:30. Once again, Frank time provided the necessary cushion. Larry pulled into the only parking spot that would be in the shade when the sun came out. A full-size red truck parked next to him.

"Charlie, you stay here and take a nap. I'll bring you breakfast in a little bit." Larry rolled all of the van windows down halfway and then reached into his pocket for a handful of jelly beans. "Here, boy, these will hold you over until I get back."

As Larry got out of the Astro, he noticed the red truck's prominent

Town and Country logo. Larry could only see the boots below the open door. When the door slammed, he connected the cowboy hat and 'RS' belt buckle. "Hello, Red, Larry Schafer with PROH$_2$O faucets!"

The Flier's neon sign shined a beam on Charlie's friendly head.

Red chuckled, "Yes, I remember you. Are you meeting Ernie here for breakfast?"

"I think it's a bit early for Ernie."

Red's eyes caught a glimpse of Charlie, who was begging for attention. "That's a good looking dog you've got in the van. You're going locking him up by himself, are you?"

"I didn't think the Flier's would approve of Charlie in the restaurant."

Red again made eye contact with Charlie. "That big old dog looks like he'll be just fine at the Flier's. Let's bring him in!"

The trio proceeded to the entrance. Charlie started sniffing as the aroma of bacon made its way through his quivering nose. Red took control, "Candy, I've got a couple of friends with me. Are we okay sitting over there in the corner?"

The timing was perfect for this kind of request because at 4:30 the Flier's was still in pre-flight mode, getting ready for business to 'take-off'. Candy smiled. "What's that big old dog's name?"

Red responded, "That's Charlie."

Candy patted Charlie on the head. "It's a pleasure to meet you. I'll assume you don't need a menu."

It was easy for anyone to like Charlie, but his charm was really a hit with the ladies. As Charlie plopped down, his eyes met Candy's, triggering another pat on the head. "Red, are you having the usual?"

After Red smiled and nodded, Candy turned to Larry. "You want a minute to check out the menu?"

Larry responded quickly, "Oh no, I'll have what Red is having!"

Candy again turned her attention to Charlie. "I'll find you something special!"

Larry started the conversation, "Red, I really appreciate you taking care of Charlie."

"So how old is he anyway?"

"Not exactly sure. We rescued him from the pound right before doomsday. Our best guess is that he's about twelve."

"I don't think I've ever seen a salesman go to work with their dog."

"Well, I've scheduled the day to visit jobsites to evaluate opportunities for our product. If you don't mind, I'd like to ask you a question."

"Is this a five dollar question or a hundred dollar question?"

"Well, it's a hundred dollar question for me, but probably a five dollar question for you. How many houses does your best finish plumber set in one day?"

When home builders develop tracts of homes by the dozens, contractors set up production schedules that call for specialists to complete the various segments of construction. For example, a plumbing contractor, like Town and Country, would have specialized crews doing prefabrication of water, gas, and sewer lines. Then he would have crews that would install that product on the job. At the end of the job, a 'finish man' installs the water heater, faucets, toilets, and other accessories.

Red responded, "Well, it kind of depends on the house, but we budget two houses a day."

"What if they don't finish two houses?"

"That's not an option. My finish plumbers don't go home until they do two houses a day!"

Larry was intrigued. "So you pay your men hourly and then overtime if needed?"

"We hate paying overtime, but to stay on schedule, we bite the bullet. Some of our competitors pay their men on piece work. The finish man might get paid $75-$100 per house, regardless of how much time is spent doing the job."

"That would sure control your costs, wouldn't it?"

"Yes, but piece work can hurt the quality of work short term and the control of your business down the road."

"Makes sense to me."

"I like happy builders! When my builders are happy, I'm happy!"

"Absolutely!"

"Larry, I need to keep an eye on you. You're pretty tricky. That was no five dollar question!"

"Really?"

"No way! Our friend Candy, she asks five dollar questions!"

Candy returned with a bowl full of left-over goodies for Charlie in one hand and a hot coffee pot in the other. As she filled the cups, she commented, "Fellas, yours will be right up. I just wanted to make sure the bacon was extra crispy."

Larry took a sip. "So, Red, you've built quite a business. What's the secret to your success?"

"I've always said that the secret to outdoing your competitors is to be less screwed-up than they are!"

"I like that! You acknowledge that your people will make mistakes, but minimizing them is the key!"

"That's about it. Football coaches preach the same thing. And sure enough, the game is usually won by the team that has the fewest turnovers!"

As Charlie licked the bottom of the bowl, Candy brought Red and Larry their breakfasts: bacon and eggs over easy, with biscuits and gravy.

"So, Red, how many people do you have working for you?"

"As far as I can tell, about half of them!"

Both men burst out into a gut-busting laugh that shook the very foundation of Flier's café. Charlie covered his ears with his paws.

"When I first met you at the shop, I noticed your belt buckle. Can you tell me about it?"

"Sure, but hang on a quick second."

Red stood and pulled the buckle off his belt. Now seated, Red continued, "This buckle belonged to my father. When he passed away, he left behind three things; a mattress full of wrinkled one dollar bills, a big smile, and this belt buckle. Since his name was Rodney, our initials are the same. Every morning when I put on this belt, who do you think I think of?"

Red handed Larry the buckle. It was forged brass. The 'R' and 'S' were framed by a star, which was fitted into a rectangular buckle. "This buckle reminds me of my father, but also reminds me that it's the little things in life that matter most!"

"Like jelly beans?"

Red had a puzzled look. Having a conversation with Larry was like maneuvering through an obstacle course. "I think you have some pipes crossed in your head! Jelly beans?"

Larry paused before he replied, "Maybe you haven't heard about the *Jelly Beans in Life*!"

Red looked at Larry through the corner of his eye, shook his head, and finally smiled.

Larry could not believe his good fortune. He was having breakfast with Red Starr, the owner of Town and Country Plumbing, the largest, most successful plumbing contractor in Southern California, and perhaps the country. On top of that, Red was a bright, practical businessman. More than that, Red was one hell of a guy!

"Larry, you make quick impulsive decisions. What would you have done if you didn't like my breakfast?"

"Take a look at this body. The chances of you ordering something I didn't like were pretty slim. But these biscuits and gravy are pretty darn good!"

"You have an interesting shuffle when you walk."

"I wish I didn't, but I sure do. Some people in our business call me Ratchet-Ass."

Red laughed. "Ratchet-Ass? Really?"

"Ah, yeah."

"Okay, 'Ratchet-Ass' I think I get it."

As the two men finished their breakfast, Candy refilled their coffee cups while Red patted Charlie on the head. "What do you think, Charlie, wasn't it better to have breakfast in here, instead of sitting in that van by yourself?"

Charlie was sound asleep and missed Red's comment.

"So Larry, are you related to the Schafer lady that's on the Lake Mathias City Council?"

"That's Susan, my wife."

"Hmmm. Does she have any idea what will be done about the moratorium?"

"She says that the will of the people will determine the outcome."

"What in the hell does that mean?"

"I'm pretty good at faucets and winning battles in the business world, but women puzzle me. Maybe you can help me figure it out."

As the two men stood, Larry reached for the bill, but Red beat him to it. "Larry, breakfast for you and Charlie is on me; but I do agree that plumbing is a lot easier to figure out than women."

Red reached down and patted Charlie on his head again. "I'll see you again old friend. Take good care of 'Ratchet-Ass' and help him figure out women. That will earn you a big juicy bone."

The two men shook hands, "Are you sure I can't buy, Red?"

"Nope, I'm saving you for a big check yet to come!"

As Red walked out, Larry talked with Candy, slipped five dollars into her hand, and returned to his table for another cup of coffee. Charlie was huddled in the corner still sound asleep.

From where Larry was sitting, he had a perfect view of the front door. It was now 5:45, and right on cue, Chip walked in. Candy directed him to Larry's table.

"Hi, Chip, do you remember me, Larry, with PROH$_2$O faucets."

"Oh yeah, sure I do! You bought me breakfast right here at the Flier's!"

"You got it, Chip, and I'm going to buy you breakfast again!"

Candy winked at Larry and smiled at Charlie. "Okay Chip, what are you having today?"

Chip ordered French toast as Candy poured him a cup of coffee.

Larry had set the stage perfectly. Now it was time to go to work. "What does your day look like, Chip?"

"Well, first thing after breakfast, I need to head to the Golden Horizons job."

Larry put his new found knowledge right to work. "How hard will it be to set two houses of finish today?"

"It'll be tough! I need to put Roman tub valves on the tubs today. That's always a time killer!"

"How many days a week do you work overtime to finish those two houses a day?"

"For me it's once or twice a week, but for some finish guys it's three or four days a week."

Larry stayed in control. "Are the guys milking it, or is it that hard to set two houses a day?"

"Red has a pretty good team. The best plumbers all want to work for him. He pays a good wage and gives everybody a fair shake."

"Chip, if you don't mind, I'd like to follow you to the job and check things out."

"Okay by me, but when we get there, I'll be super busy, so I won't have much time to talk to you."

"No worries, you may even find that I'll be a help, not a hindrance."

While Chip slammed down his breakfast, Larry slipped Candy cash to cover Chip's breakfast and a Charlie sized tip. The day was off to a great start! Without Candy, everything would have been different. She had no idea how much she was appreciated.

Larry and Charlie followed Chip out the door and down the road. The homebuilder of the Golden Horizons job, Cedar Wood Developers, was the largest builder in the county. Billboard after billboard advertised the project. The message was clear: only fools would pass on the opportunity to live in the Golden Horizons master planned community! Larry didn't need to follow Chip to the job; following the signs would have done the trick.

Forty-seven signs later, Chip's pick-up truck and Larry's Astro pulled into the project, and wiggled around a variety of equipment to lot 23, where they parked. Larry brought a toolbox filled with parts, samples, and a few handy tools. He pointed to a spot in the corner of the garage, and out of harm's way. "Charlie, you stay here!"

Chip, now on his home turf, barked out orders, "Let's make sure everything is ready for finish!"

The men walked through the two story house, bottom to top, end to end before Chip declared it was a go. Everything was ready. The faucets, toilets, water heater, and installation accessories were all in the garage, organized and ready. Chip told Larry that he liked to set the toilets first and proceeded to take them to their respective bathrooms. While Chip worked on the toilets, Larry went to work on the water heater. He located a box cutter from his tool box. In a flash, he had the water heater on its stand in the garage. He connected the flexible gas and water connectors with a wrench, snapped on the draft diverter and connected the vent pipe. The final step was to plumb a piece of PVC pipe and elbow to the safety valve. To earn extra cash, Larry had installed water heaters many times with Big Ben. He had no idea at that time that those experiences would impact him today and tomorrow. Ben had tried to explain the life lesson to Larry in Ventura standing over a pipe threading machine, but young ears do not always listen.

About an hour later, Chip returned to the garage. "You guys are still here?"

"Of course!"

"Well Larry, I'm not sure why you are killing a day here, but as I told you, I won't have a lot of time for you. The next step is to get the water heater on its stand and connected."

Chip looked down at the cardboard box on the ground. Then he turned around and saw that the water heater had been installed. "Holy shit! Was that really your handy work?"

Larry answered the question brimming with confidence and pride, "No, actually, it was Charlie."

"I thought you said you were a faucet salesman."

"I am, but I've spent lots of time in a plumbing shop. Did I do Okay?"

Chip inspected Larry's installation. "On the water connector, did you use plumber's putty?"

"Of course not! The rubber gasket that makes the seal would leak if you put putty on it."

"You're the first salesman I've ever met that really knows plumbing. Okay, let's see how good you are at installing kitchen faucets."

"Sounds like I just got hired!"

The two men took the sink out of a box and easily installed the basket strainer, air gap, and garbage disposer. The final step was to install the Alpha single lever faucet. Larry had heard all over the territory that Alpha was famous for not packing all the parts into their boxes.

"Damn it, Larry, the Alpha sons-of-bitches forgot to supply the mounting hardware that holds the son-of-a-bitch to the sink!"

"To be honest with you, we also forget to pack stuff in a box sometimes. That's why I provide plumbers buying my product a big toolbox loaded with handles, screws, handle extensions, hold-down hardware, etc. Does Alpha do that for you?"

"Yeah right, Larry. I've been pissing and moaning about this to Ernie forever, but nothing ever happens. I've robbed parts out of boxes all over this job. It drives me crazy and kills lots of time. Alright, enough of that, I'll get back to this kitchen after I set the rest of the finish. Who knows, I may need some other parts. Thanks for setting the water heater for me; that really saved my ass!"

The lavatory faucets were next. There was no problem with the parts on the faucet, but the pop-up assemblies were difficult, at best. Larry showed Chip a sample of a $PROH_2O$ pop-up designed with a polypropylene snap together feature that could be installed in half the time. A pop-up consists of the sink drain that is operated by moving the rod behind the faucet up or down.

"Damn, Larry, I like that pop-up. Are you sure it doesn't leak. It looks too good to be true!"

"No product is perfect, but plumbers tell me they have fewer call backs on this pop-up because the linkage is so dialed-in!"

The men headed to the Roman tub faucet that required an eight-inch spout to be twisted onto a threaded pipe. Chip was a good plumber. He spun and cranked the massive spout around in circles until it was finally tight. Then, he used the leverage of the spout to crank it really hard so that it would be mounted in the proper direction. "I always worry about that last turn. Sometimes I break loose the fitting, which triggers a service call, which costs the company money, and makes me look bad!"

Larry showed Chip the PROH$_2$O design. The spout slipped over a smooth brass pipe. The seal was made with an 'O' Ring and the assembly was tightened securely with a set screw.

Chip beamed. "I love it. If you guys were smart, you would also use that design on the diverter tub spout. The Alpha design is also a pain in the ass on that spout!"

"Already done, Chip. We introduced a slip-fit diverter spout two years ago. The Roman tub idea came from the regular tub spout."

"Larry, if I was the purchasing agent, I would switch to your product in a heartbeat. Unfortunately, I'm just a plumber. You definitely need to talk to Ernie."

"I tried that, but Ernie won't talk to me. Maybe I should go straight to Red. What do you think?"

"If Ernie won't talk to you, how in the hell do you think you'll get a chance to talk to Red?"

"Don't worry about that part, I'll figure out the rest. Thanks for letting me come to the job. Charlie and I are heading out. If you run into Red, you might mention what you think of our product."

"By the way, you were right. You were a help and not a hindrance. But Larry, I didn't think you were trying to sell me on anything, but you ended up selling me on just about everything!"

CHAPTER 8

"Signs"

Susan's mind was perceptive. Her tongue was sharp. Her eyes were keen. And her ears missed nothing and heard everything.

"Susan can hear snails crawl," Larry would mumble.

It was a late Friday night, inching its way towards Saturday. Charlie was snoring on one side of Susan and Larry on the other. In the gaps between the two fog horns blowing, Susan heard a noise not in harmony with the snoring or Mother Nature. The sound was not crickets chirping, owls hooting or that of any other creature. Likewise, the sound was different from the typical man-made sounds that carried through the still of any ranch night from distant highways.

Annie Oakley Road was the dirt road that terminated at Penny Lane. Since that intersection was the end of both roads, it was rarely traveled by anyone, except Larry and Susan, or a visiting friend. There were a handful of ranch-style homes with Annie Oakley addresses in Lake

Mathias, but cars heading to those destinations turned off far before the end of the dirt road at 'The Ranch'.

Susan sprang straight up from her deep sleep. She could hear a slow moving truck and then a door creaking open, ever so slowly. This was followed by a pounding sound. She turned her head to zero-in on the disturbance. Was that the sound of a sledge hammer pounding a stake? Surely, it couldn't be a neighbor mending a fence. Not in the middle of the night. That wouldn't make sense. Susan shook Larry and retrieved him from the world of the dead. He bolted up and mumbled words that only the dying would utter to the already dead. She whispered to him as he rubbed his eyes and squarely shook his head, "Listen! Do you hear those sounds?"

Larry heard nothing. Silence…nothing! Actually, at that moment, Susan heard nothing. The pounding had suddenly stopped. Then came another door slam, followed by the sound of a truck racing back down Annie Oakley Road. Larry looked outside the bedroom window and watched tail lights fade into the distance. Susan listened until the sound disappeared into a more typical Lake Mathias silence.

"Susan, it's just someone who made a wrong turn, got lost, and then got themselves un-lost."

"Nobody gets themselves lost in the middle of nowhere, in the middle of the night, at 'The Ranch'. We better check this thing out!"

Charlie slept through the disturbance. As Susan crawled out of bed, he finally gathered there was something up. His ears half-heartedly stood at a sleepy attention. Was Susan just going to the bathroom, or was something really going on? When Larry moved slowly from his side of the bed, Charlie determined that something WAS up. By the time Larry got to the hall, every light in the house was on and Susan took command. "I don't see any signs of trouble in here. Let's walk down Penny Lane to where the noise was coming from!"

Larry thought that was a really dumb idea, but also knew that there was no way to talk Susan out of this investigation. It was the kind of pitch dark night that black cats only dream of. Since there were no street lights in this part of Lake Mathias, only the twinkle of stars and the beam of the flashlight guided them through the darkness. Larry was cautious. Susan was determined. Charlie sniffed a zigzag route not sure what they were looking for. A trip to the bottom of Penny Lane found the gate locked and no signs of any trouble.

It was now 1:05 AM. Since the investigation drew a blank, by 1:10 AM the detectives were back in bed. The snorers were snoring to Susan's north and south and after a few moments of restless nesting, Susan also fell fast asleep.

Night turned peacefully into day as the bright June sun pierced through the window of the master bedroom. Susan rubbed her eyes and again nudged Larry, who jumped up from yet another intrusion of his sleep. "Now what?"

"It's your lucky day. You get to ride in my Corvette and buy me breakfast!"

Larry's bobbling head wobbled until it slammed back down onto his pillow. Susan got up and headed for the shower. Larry's short night of sleep was not rewarded with sleeping in. To the contrary, Susan had declared there would be a road trip.

By the time Larry got out of the bathroom, Susan had slipped a yellow sun dress over her wet hair.

"Where are we going?"

"On a road trip!"

"Am I taking you, or are you taking me?"

"Larry, I am not riding in your Astro!"

"How about Charlie?"

"You know the answer to that!"

Larry patted Charlie on his old, sad, head. "Looks like you get to stay home."

Charlie lazily wagged his tail. After the night's drama, he was all for being 'Master of The Ranch' while napping on the front porch.

It took Larry no time to get ready. In just a few scrambled flashes, his teeth were scrubbed, morning beard shaven, and hair shampooed. His outfit was typical for a square head like Larry: flip-flops, shorts, and a Hawaiian shirt that only a tourist would wear. He patted Charlie on the head. "Signs on the walls inside my head are warning me to keep my eyes wide open today. It's becoming apparent that it won't be easy for me to be me today!"

Susan's rules dictated that Charlie was not allowed to ride in the Corvette because of the hairy mess he left behind and Larry was not allowed to drive her sports car. The painful truth was that, in their early years, Larry never let Susan drive his Volkswagen, so now Larry was enduring a forever payback. The males at 'The Ranch' were definitely subject to the rules and regulations set by management.

Susan had a happy smile as she slipped gracefully behind the wheel. The Corvette was like a wild lion from the jungle that needed to be tamed, and she was the trainer. She started the engine. The machine's 327 horse power motor broke the quiet of the ranch morning with a hellacious, robust roar. In preparation for the ride in the topless sports car, her wet hair was tied into a pony-tail. The Corvette crept down Penny Lane like a ranch tarantula looking for prey. As Larry waived to Charlie, Susan screamed. As he turned his head forward, the cause of the scream and the noise heard the previous night, was right there before him! At the dead-end corner of Penny Lane and Annie Oakley, there was a sign. Not just any sign, but a sign that felt like the sting of a ranch scorpion. The Corvette screeched to a sliding stop on the dirt road. The sign was three feet wide and two feet high. "SQUASHED HOUSING EQUALS GHOST TOWN."

"Larry, that's what was going on last night. People have a lot of damn nerve putting a sign on the corner of our property!"

Susan shifted into first gear and hit the gas so hard that a dust storm exploded behind them. Then, just as quickly, she slammed on the brake! "What, in the world, is going on? Who's tormenting me with this sign campaign? Larry! You and I are going to find out!"

A silent steaming followed. When Susan was quiet, trouble was brewing! Larry wanted to comment, but at a moment like this, no need to throw more logs into the inferno.

"Larry, I bet home builders are responsible! They have a lot of nerve planting a sign in front of our house. If they're trying to sway my vote to end the moratorium, they're going about it the wrong damn way!"

First silence, then profanity! The signs in Larry's head flashed a red neon message, 'Danger Ahead!'

A smoking hot Susan now stormed from the driver's side to Larry's side. She opened Larry's door and handed him the keys. "I'm too irritated to drive!"

Larry got into the driver's seat and stopped. He was conflicted. He was excited about driving the Corvette, but not under these circumstances.

"What are you waiting for?"

"Maybe we should go home and have a cup of coffee topped with a shot of Bailey's Irish Cream, to calm things down a bit."

"Larry, we are going to take a road trip. We are going to find out about this sign business. And, we are going to have fun!"

Larry muttered to himself, "Somehow this isn't shaping up to be a fun day!" His private thoughts were that only Susan could screw-up his first shot at driving the Corvette. "So where are we going?"

"To Sunnymeade! I want to see how builders destroy small towns!"

"I think we both need a cup of coffee to clear our heads and think straight!"

"Then we'll get coffee in Sunnymeade. I'm certain you know of a restaurant where we can have coffee!"

"As a matter of fact, I do. In fact, I know just the place: Flier's Café."

With a heavy sigh Susan replied, "You're right, I do need a strong, strong cup of coffee!"

Larry moved the gear shift to first, and then second. Because, seated next to him was a stick of dynamite disguised as a beautiful woman in a sun dress, he proceeded with reluctant caution. He had never seen Susan this worked-up about anything. He started piecing together a plan to get things settled down, but first he needed to think things through.

Investors likely owned much of the undeveloped land in Lake

Mathias. Some of those investors were probably builders. The best way to maximize a return on their investment in the land would be for the moratorium to be dropped. Overnight, the value would sky-rocket. It might be logical for those investors to fund a campaign that would influence the council's decision. The disposition of the moratorium would be decided by the town council the last Wednesday in July. That was right around the corner. Larry had kept himself on the sideline. He and Susan had wrestled with the topic, and men like Red had brought it up, but for the most part, Larry had kept clear of the subject. However, a sign had just changed everything. The remainder of the month would certainly be interesting. Life with Susan under this kind of scrutiny and pressure might at times be torturous. Indeed, everyday might be Wednesday for much of the hot summer.

"Larry, I feel like a dusty tumbleweed rolling through a swamp. My hair feels like I just took a mud bath. Look at my car! Look at my dress!"

"I'm not sure, but it may have something to do with that sign. That sign turned you into an irritated driver, with wet hair, on a dirt road. That's a sticky combination. I'm not a chemist, but I'm pretty sure that dust plus water equals mud. Let's go back to 'The Ranch' for a shower and a Bailey's. Shoot, we can forget about the coffee and just hit the Bailey's!"

The thorns of Susan's tumbleweed explosion now dug into Larry's skin. "No-way! You're not getting out of this that easy! Easy, that's what you like! Oh no, we're not doing this the easy way! We're going on our road trip and we're going to find out whose idea it was to aggravate me with that sign. When I get to that sign S.O.B., there will be hell to pay!"

The dusty '58 Corvette was now approaching the corner of Annie Oakley and Lake Mathias Drive.

Susan shrieked as if she was watching an Alfred Hitchcock movie.

Larry stopped the car. Round two was now in full swing. On each corner of the intersection were more signs. The messages were like missiles aimed at Susan's head.

"KIDS NEED BALLFIELDS NOT MORATORIUMS."

"COMMON SENSE TRUMPS NONSENSE"

"SMALL TOWN POLITICS WON'T PAY YOUR BILLS"

"Larry, if they want war, they better be ready! They should have never picked a fight with me!"

Larry turned north onto Lake Mathias Road. As they proceeded, the population of signs became a forest of messages. There was a sign on each side of the street every 30 yards, as far as the eye could see.

It was a million signs verses one Susan. Larry didn't like the odds. Susan could handle almost anything, but a million signs, fighting one fuming woman, was a mismatch. Larry kept his analysis inside his square head. "Whenever I have a bad day, Charlie licks me in the face, I pat his head, and then we both feel better. I guess I need to be Charlie."

"Susan, these signs won't kill you. You said the will of the people would determine the outcome of the moratorium. Well, the people will now hear one point of view from these damn signs. That doesn't mean they will agree with them! I suspect that it'll be standing room only at the big council meeting. People will voice their opinions. Some people are happy with what they've got, and others will want what they think they're missing. That's life!"

Susan stared out the window as they passed more and more signs. She turned her head towards Larry. She smiled as she sized him up from the bottom of his big clumsy feet to the top of his square head. The head alone was worth noting. His hair was like an orchestra all playing from different sheets of music. Plus, half of the musicians had tragically disappeared.

She smiled. Larry's square head was mounted upon a stretched torso framed by a set of wide hips, and short, well-defined Popeye legs. His shirts were always too short and his pants too long.

No, Susan did not marry Larry because he was artfully sculptured. And, since they met when he was flat broke, it cannot be said she married him for his money. All in all, she married him because she loved him.

She often wondered why she loved him. But the fact of the matter was that through all their verbal ping pong slams to the corner, life with Larry was never, ever boring. And, when the signs were up and the chips were down, he was there, standing beside her. He was her Don Quixote! If windmills or signs needed to be slain, Larry would always be there to fight them with her.

She softly stroked Larry's right hand as he precisely shifted the Corvette's gear shifter. Then she rubbed a muddy tear as it rolled down her cheek.

Larry had carved a spot in Susan's heart because he made her laugh. Even on days when she wanted to kill him, he would find ways to make her laugh. No, that laughter was not always expressed outwardly, but secretly Larry made her body tingle throughout her insides. Larry had that effect when they first shared a cup of coffee at Ventura College, and now, as they headed for their next cup of coffee sixteen years later, he still made her tingle inside. "Larry! Please stop the car!"

Larry pulled to the side of the road between signs. He turned his head to see mud trails streaming from Susan's wet, crusted eyes. As jelly bean shaped tears slid down her dusty cheeks, she shook her head. Larry smiled and gave her a wink. She had never before been this vulnerable and this beautiful. The signs that triggered her fiery rage gave her a red glow that framed muddy tears. "Oh Larry, thank you for understanding! I love you!"

The road trippers kissed a long kiss that made them feel like passionate Ventura College sweethearts. Only the gear shifter separated them. Larry was bewildered. Was this a sign of things yet to be? His mind entered a fantasyland. Where had they been? Where were they now? In hopes of restoring reality, he shook himself! Where were they going? Susan looked into Larry's spaced-out eyes. Seeking to restore order, she made a plea, "Larry! Larry! Is anybody home? Hello!" Larry was startled! He returned to the world of the living and smiled, concluding that, at that splinter of a moment, life with Susan was good; torturously crazy, but nonetheless good.

CHAPTER 9

"Zwischengas"

L arry loved shifting the Corvette from second to third. As the stick shift traveled through neutral, he revved up the RPMs by hitting the gas sharply. Papa had taught him this technique. Papa called it 'zwischengas'; translated from German to English in two parts; 'zwischen' means 'between' and 'gas' is 'gas' (in either language). A close pronunciation for 'zwischengas' is 'swish-en-gas'.

When Larry drove his VW in Ventura, he also shifted with 'zwischengas'. Unfortunately, that 'zwischengas', powered by a dreadfully weak 1200cc motor, was embarrassingly wimpy; so wimpy that Susan never noticed. But in the Corvette, he felt like he was driving on the Ontario speedway, looking for the checkered flag. 'Zwischengas' fueled his love for both driving and his departed father, hero, and friend: Papa.

Papa taught Larry and his brother, Otto, many life lessons. He taught them how to compete and win, the importance of being fiercely independent, and how to be precise with all things mathematical, from measurements to bowling scores.

Larry's first job, at the age of nine, was keeping score for Papa's bowling team. Each bowler paid him a quarter. The job required a quick mind and impeccable accuracy. Larry became a scorekeeper, four years after the family immigrated from Germany with two suitcases, a handful of unpaid bills, and huge dreams for a better life.

The ping pong table in the backyard provided a place to cultivate the competitive spirit. Because the sound of the ball volleying back and forth made the sound of 'ka-nip-ka-nop', Papa, Larry, and Otto called the game exactly that: 'ka-nip-ka-nop'! Years later, Larry taught Susan how to play the game and how to play it to win.

Papa also taught Larry how to be tough. When he was seven, a bee stung the donkey Larry was riding. The bucking donkey sent Larry straight up and straight down, landing him on his forehead. There was not much damage to the gravel road, but Larry's forehead split wide open. Otto, who was riding a horse, hurried Larry to the surgeon, who of course was Papa. Since Papa was a machinist, his tool box included a pair of needle nose tweezers. Papa wiped off the blood with a wet rag and then removed the particles of gravel from the wound, one granule at a time. He then wiped it with alcohol. A bandage completed the job. Five minutes later, to provide a diversion, Larry and Otto put their baseball mitts on and played a game of catch.

Larry and Otto were brothers and best friends. The brothers walked from their rural home in Topanga Canyon, about a mile to the school bus stop with their dog Lassie at their side. When the bus returned at 3:30, Lassie was there to greet them. The rural area was much like Lake Mathias, so it was easy to understand how Larry was attracted to 'The Ranch'.

The two brothers had a love affair with baseball. They listened to Dodger games on their transistor radio and were mesmerized by the voice of Vin Scully. The legendary broadcaster painted word pictures of Sandy Koufax striking out Willie Mays with a 'dazzling' curveball, Don Drysdale throwing a 'high-hard-one' at Willie McCovey's head, and Maury Wills reaching base on a bunt before stealing yet another base. The hypnotic voice and magical words taught Larry and Otto about baseball and, more importantly, about the gritty determination required to succeed in life.

Larry and Otto fought, argued, and played much like any brothers growing up. Larry, being the little brother, drove Otto crazy at times, perhaps most of the time. It was not unusual to hear Otto scream at Larry to, 'act normal'!

Papa taught Larry about 'zwischengas', but he also taught him the inner satisfactions that love for animals can bring, especially dogs. The only thing that Papa was unable to teach Larry was the art of understanding women. Larry was in a long line of Schafer males confused by females. Papa engineered tooling for a key instrument that landed the first man on the moon. But reverse engineering the thought processes of women seemed impossible to him. He searched for answers everywhere. When he really got frustrated, he would go into the garage and find a hidden bottle of gin. Based on Papa's results, Larry was certain that there were no revelations found in gin bottles, either.

"Larry, what are you doing to my car?"

"I'm driving, and boy is it fun!"

"Don't get used to it. I'm still getting even with you for not letting me drive your VW. Anyway, it's obvious you have a love affair with your van."

"You've been punishing me for 16 years! Anyway, the Astro is a man's truck that serves a manly purpose!"

"Oh, like going to the dump, I suppose."

Larry shifted from third gear to fourth using 'zwischengas' between the gears, "I'm still dying for that cup of coffee!"

"You just did it again!"

"What?"

"The gas, Larry! The gas! You're doing something funny with the gas!"

"That's just zwischengas!"

"What?"

"Never mind Susan, we're almost to the Flier's Café."

"Perfect! I need to get cleaned up and then I'll be ready for that cup of coffee you promised me."

Larry and Susan were having quite a day. The road trip had turned into an adventure. In less than an hour, their day shifted gears much like the Corvette. First gear accelerated quickly into 'sign-ology', the study of the annoying signs that challenged Susan to identify her tormentor. In second gear, Larry and Susan rediscovered wanderlust on the side of a highway between signs, separated only by a gear shifter. And now, as they headed down the highway, they were invigorated by the wind blowing around their muddy hair as Larry shifted into fourth gear using 'zwischengas'.

Once they arrived in Sunnymeade, the signs stopped and the billboards started. "Well Larry, those signs really got to me. I'm glad we're past them. But now we're being bombarded with giant signs designed to convince people that traffic, smog, and crowds create prosperity. I just don't get it."

"They're just trying to sell houses."

"That's the first thing you've said to me that makes any sense at all. That 'zwischengas' nonsense is as crazy as these signs."

"Flier's is just ahead. Finally, we'll get that cup of coffee."

Larry couldn't believe the Flier's parking lot. It was as busy as the county fair on opening day. He had never been to the Flier's on a Saturday. He thought that it would be less popular on weekends because most construction sites were shut down on Saturdays and Sundays. He was wrong. "Maybe we should find another place. The Flier's is packed!"

"The only place where I like crowds is at restaurants. A restaurant without a crowd is a bad restaurant. This must be a great restaurant. Please park the car, I think I like the Flier's already!"

Larry headed to the back of the lot where a car was pulling out. As Larry pulled into the spot a red truck stared straight ahead at them. The license plate confirmed it. 'REDSTAR'.

"Susan, this place is going to be crazy, let's find another restaurant!"

Larry's worst nightmare would be for Red to meet Susan. That could result in trouble, lots of trouble!

"Don't be silly. This will be fun. I've been angry all day. I'm ready for some fun!"

As they walked into the chaotic restaurant they were greeted by Candy, who was serving up fresh coffee from the pots she held in both hands. "I'll be right with you, Larry. Where's Charlie?"

"Larry, don't tell me you brought Charlie in here. The health department would have had a field day. You're embarrassing me!"

"Charlie was a big hit here. And neither one of us was arrested."

"How many times have you been here?"

"This is my third time."

"You must be a big tipper. The waitress sure knows who you are!"

"That's Candy. She's amazing!"

Candy worked her way back to Larry and Susan. "You must be Mrs. Larry. You are one lucky woman. If you ever get tired of Larry, let me know. I'll take him off your hands!"

Susan was momentarily speechless, but then fired back, "Okay, Candy, I'll certainly keep that in mind."

"As you guys can see we're standing room only, but I found a perfect spot. Follow me." Candy led the Schafers to a table in the corner with two empty seats. The man in the third seat stood and smiled, "Hey there Ratchet-ass!"

Susan's emotions bounced like the stock market on a volatile day.

"And you must be Susan. My name is Red. I am very pleased to meet you. Larry is a very lucky guy. Don't tell me you left Charlie in the van?"

Larry smiled as he sat down. As Susan excused herself to use the restroom, she commented, "I love that star buckle, Red."

Larry sighed, "Charlie's at home! On our road trip this morning, I revved up my wife's Corvette using 'zwischengas'! And Susan's recovering from the attack of a million signs and rinsing the mud out of her hair! It's been a great Saturday! How the heck are you doing?"

"You sure have a way with words!"

"By the way Red, after we had breakfast last week, I hooked up with your finish man, Chip."

"Oh, I heard all about it. The Chipper gave me a full report. If I was interested in switching faucets, we definitely would be talking!"

"I appreciate that Red. I know you're not interested, but I need a favor. Please allow me to come in and tell you about our whole program. At least that way you'll know what programs we're capable of offering your competitors. Win, lose or draw, we can still be friends and have breakfast here at the Flier's!"

"You've got a deal! Call me when you're ready to talk."

Candy and Susan returned to the table at the same time. As Candy poured the coffee, Larry stared at Susan. She looked as fresh as a hand-picked ranch peach. She had magically transformed herself into the Susan he fell in love with, oh so long ago. Her hair was glowing, her lips were painted a bright red that matched Red's truck, and the makeover seemed to have invigorated her. Larry was flabbergasted!

Candy was ready for business. "Okay, Larry, you want your usual, just like Red?"

"That was a good guess!"

"And how about you, Mrs. Larry?"

"Well, let me see. To begin with my name is Susan. I think I'll go with the French toast."

"Gotcha covered Susan. Do you want the combo with your eggs poached?"

"That would be perfect. How did you know I like my eggs poached?"

"Just a guess!"

Susan grabbed her cup and sipped that first sip of coffee, that she desperately needed. "My, oh my, that's great coffee. Red, it is very nice to meet you. I can see you and Larry have become good pals. What brings you here to the Flier's?"

"I live right up the road. My farm is now a plumbing shop and I live in the old farm house at the back of the property. I lead a very boring life that mainly consists of plumbing, the Flier's, and now Larry. When the pressure really gets to me, I shoot my shotgun at flying skeet!"

"That sounds fine as long as you don't shoot Larry," said Susan.

Red replied, "I've never shot one salesman. I've had a couple of plumbers that nearly got shot, but so far salesmen have been safe. Of course, I really don't talk to salesmen. My purchasing agent deals with salesmen."

Susan laughed and said, "Red, let me introduce you to Larry. He's a salesman!"

"Really? I thought his name was Ratchet-Ass," said Red. "So Ratchet-Ass, are you really a salesman? If you are, I need you to talk to Ernie!"

Larry posed a question: "Have I tried to sell you anything, yet?"

Red replied quickly, "I think the key word was 'yet'!"

"Didn't I just train Charlie to sleep in this corner," posed Larry.

"It was really hard to teach him how to sleep," teased Red.

"See, I'm a dog trainer," said Larry. "Thanks for helping me out with Charlie last week."

Susan was intrigued. She enjoyed watching Larry the salesman in action with a customer. He was having fun with Red and Red was having fun with him. Red's laugh vibrated as robustly as the 327 in the Corvette. "So what brings you guys to the Flier's?"

Susan quickly responded, "We followed the trail of signs from small ones with big teeth, to gigantic ones, with happy pictures of lives fulfilled when a house is purchased in Sunnymeade!"

"I've seen the billboards with happy kids in big yards, living in two story houses with green lawns. I don't think I've seen the small signs."

Larry watched as Susan responded, "The small ones were erected in a trail that started in front of our house and extended all the way to Sunnymeade!"

"What do they say?"

"That only fools would prevent Lake Mathias from becoming the next Sunnymeade!"

"It sounds like those small signs got your attention!"

"You strike me as a smart, kind-hearted man running a successful business. Who do you think is behind these signs?"

Red smiled. "Well, it was definitely not me. I'm in the plumbing business, not the sign business. But what I've learned over the years is that, if you follow a trail of money to the end, you'll find the owner of the printing machine."

"You sound like Mayor Sam! I bet Mayor Sam would say the exact same thing!"

Red turned to Larry. "It looks like I just got on Susan's bad side. Help me out here!"

"You're fine! Susan loves Mayor Sam!"

Right on cue, Candy arrived with three plates balanced on her left arm, "Okay kids, let's see, Susan, here you go, French toast and two poached eggs; and gentlemen, the usual, bacon crispy and eggs over medium. Let me know if you need more gravy for the biscuits. I'll be right back with some more coffee!"

Susan was invigorated. "Looks absolutely scrumptious. I feel like I'm crashing a private party, but I'm absolutely loving it! Thanks for letting me into your secret club!"

Candy returned with more coffee and handed Larry a doggy bag. "This is for Charlie!"

Susan returned to the business at hand. "So Red, what do you like better, the old Sunnymeade or the new Sunnymeade?"

"You're just like Larry, throwing out twenty dollar questions! The next one you ask me will cost you!"

"What will it cost me, a bag of jelly beans?"

"Great guess! How did you know?"

"Well, if you'll recall, I am married to Larry!"

Red continued, "Let me see. I guess I would have to say that I don't care much for either one because they're not by the ocean! I love the ocean! It's way too hot and dusty out here! I would say the old Sunnymeade was too small and boring and the new one is too cookie cutter. Now don't get me wrong, I'm a business man and the construction of Sunnymeade has been real good for my wallet and my employees, but in a perfect world, I would live in an old town near the beach where an old cowboy would be welcome. I've been to Newport Beach, but it doesn't seem to be the kind of place that's partial to old cowboys!"

Larry jumped into the mix. "Exactly, Red! Ventura is the place. Not too big, not too small. Not too hot, not too cold. It's full of history and there are spots on the water just waiting for old cowboys!"

"I thought you were a dog trainer, not a realtor!" As he turned towards Susan, Red chuckled like a high school kid with a crush on his teacher. "Okay, Mrs. Town Council Woman. I know those signs irritated you a tad, but put them aside a minute and be objective. What do you think the council will decide?"

"We're at a crossroads. Speaking as a citizen of Lake Mathias, I don't like cookie cutter. If I wanted cookie cutter, I'd live in the new Sunnymeade. But the decision is not about me; it's about what the town wants. The next town council meeting will certainly be very interesting. Isn't it true that builders and contractors, like yourself, would stand to make money on the homebuilding, if the moratorium was eliminated?"

Susan was playing with fire. Red's face mirrored the reflection of his name. Larry wanted to intercede, but that, at best, felt awkward.

"Now you moved up to the $100 question category. Yes, some of my builders have land in Lake Mathias that they would like to develop. And yes, if they actually built homes there, we might do the plumbing on some of them. Personally, I don't pay too much attention to it. But my builders are always bringing it up. Do you guys own your home in Lake Mathias?"

Larry grinned. "Us and the bank!"

"If the experts are right, you guys will also stand to make money on the increase in home values. Susan, I don't think I would want to be in your shoes! You're damned if you do and damned if you don't. This thing is a boiling kettle of water. If you're not careful, the lid will blow off! You might consider meeting the truck halfway!"

Susan calmly responded. "So how would I meet the truck halfway?"

"If I wanted to pay $50 for an old refrigerator that was in your garage, but you wanted to get $75 for it, you could offer to deliver it to me provided I paid the $75. Some people think that the only solution is to split the price down the middle and do the deal for $62.50. Clever negotiators are smarter than that!"

Susan smiled. "So I just need to meet the truck halfway?"

"Bingo!"

As usual, Candy's timing was perfect. "You kids want anything else?"

The trio all patted their belly as if to say they were full. The truth was, their brains were fried as crisp as the bacon Candy served up.

"Okay, Ratchet, I'm sure we'll be talking. As for you, Mrs. Ratchet, I hope you're happy. You whipped this old cowboy like he was a city slicker at his first rodeo. I'm not sure what the rules are so I need to ask. If an old cowboy gave a town council woman a hug, would he get slapped?"

Susan responded with a hug that caused Candy to laugh and hand the check to Red. "Based on that hug, I'm guessing you just bought breakfast."

As they walked across the parking lot the three new friends celebrated like fourth graders at Disneyland. Red climbed in his truck and blew the horn as he drove by.

"Larry, give me the keys please. Your turn is over!"

As the Corvette pulled onto the highway, Susan shifted the Signet Red 1958 Corvette from first to second with a sharp shot of 'zwischengas' roaring between the gears. Susan and the Corvette were one. After she progressed to third and then to fourth gear, again using 'zwischengas', she lovingly squeezed Larry's hand. The wind blowing her hair wildly, seemed to blow her troubles away. The trip to the Flier's was torturously long. The return to the ranch was turbo-charged! Her heart pounded with exhilaration!

As she turned down Annie Oakley, she slowed to prevent the dust clouds that had started the day. As she down-shifted, she pushed aside the anger and replaced it with determination. The signs that filled Annie

Oakley and her head were still there, but thanks to Red, she was now armed with a strategy that could pave the way for the council to make a decision that really would be in the best interest of the town. The signs' trail of money needed to be followed! If there were improprieties, she would find out who was responsible. She needed to devise a plan that would meet the truck halfway, but today's road trip was an adventure, perhaps a revelation.

"Susan, my head is spinning. I thought Red was a contractor. It turns out he's a teacher. And you! You weren't teaching you were listening, learning and selling. As for me, I'm either a dog trainer or a realtor named Ratchet-Ass!"

CHAPTER 10

"Coffee"

After breakfast at the Flier's with Larry and Red, Susan became more determined and assertive than ever. She was always a doer, but now, on her 'sign' quest, she had shifted to fourth gear with 'zwischengas'. She was on a mission!

On Sunday she called Mayor Sam; asking him to lead a discussion on ethics as they apply to public service. Sam embraced the idea and told her he would be ready for the challenge at the Wednesday, July 22nd meeting.

It was just Saturday morning that Red had planted seeds that led Susan to develop an action plan. By Sunday night, the plan was in place. On Monday she persistently worked her way up the ladder until she got the ear of Ben Crawford, the editor of the *Riverside Gazette*, the county newspaper that served Lake Mathias residents. Mary Wilson would be doing a series of articles on the Lake Mathias building moratorium. And now, on this Tuesday, the plan was in full swing!

While a focused Susan prepared for the interview, Larry loaded his golf clubs into the back of the Astro. He and his boss, Frank, would be spending much of the day together. Larry was never crazy about sitting through torturous conference room meetings with big tables and overstuffed chairs, but a meeting with Frank on the golf course was always a great day. Woven around business talk, there would be heckling, strict enforcement of golf rules, and a friendly bet. Scorekeeping would be scrutinized like an IRS audit. There would be no 'gimmes' on the greens. Putts would be struck until the ball hit the bottom of the hole. 'Mulligans'? Not a chance! No freebees or do-overs were allowed! Every stroke counted!

"Susan, it will be a fun dinner tonight. You'll tell me all about your interview and I'll fill you in on my day with Frank!"

Larry headed down the driveway and made his right hand turn onto Annie Oakley. As he did, a royal blue muscle car with chrome wheels pulled beside him. He rolled down his window, "Sorry about the dust. Blue cars and dirt roads are a bad combination. Hi, I'm Larry Schafer. You must be here to see my wife, Susan."

"Nice to meet you, Larry, I'm Mary Wilson, with the *Riverside Gazette*. My DNA prevents me from driving slowly, but this road is a bit dusty. This trail of signs leading to your home is certainly interesting!"

"I'm quite sure that Susan will tell you all about them!"

Mary bid farewell and proceeded to 'The Ranch'.

The Jelly Beans in Mary's life were sometimes sweet, and sometimes sour. She had painfully learned that in struggling relationships the bad days outnumber the good ones. She acknowledged that her failed marriage, to a manly truck driver, was as much her fault as it was his. The net result was that she was now single. It took a while to settle into single self-reliance. Searching for love, she dated her share of winners and losers. Unfortunately the losers far outnumbered the winners, and the winners just didn't click. It became frustratingly evident that misery can be found both in and out of marriage. After one too many bad dating experiences, she finally resolved that she would no longer search for love.

If true love were to be had, it would need to find her. Once she accepted the Jelly Beans for what they were, she found a renewed peace of mind, a revitalized spirit and a rekindled zest for life.

Mary Wilson loved her job. The *Riverside Gazette* rewarded her talents by assigning her stories that required bulldogged investigative reporting. She had exposed scandals in both the private and public sectors. It was sometimes painful to get to the heart of an issue, but she was always up for the challenge.

Like a chameleon changes the color of its skin, Mary had the ability to change her personality. She always dressed for an assignment professionally, but kept a casual wardrobe in her car. If the opportunity presented itself and she was comfortable with the integrity of the interviewee, she would slip into her relaxed outfit to 're-set the table'. This technique typically changed the course of a conversation for the better.

Likewise, Mary would drink her coffee black until she was at ease with the direction of the story and knew that the question-answer session was sincere and honest; even brutally honest. When that occurred, and only then, Mary would add a splash of milk to make her smile and a sprinkle of sugar to make her sweet.

As she turned up Penny Lane, she determined that job one was to determine if Susan Schafer was part of the problem or the cornerstone of the solution. Was she a councilwoman being paid by special interests to divisively set the course of a town, or was she that rare honest politician?

Mary was suspicious of the trail of signs that led to the Schafer's home. The signs seemed to indicate that the councilwoman was adamantly in favor of ending the moratorium. Why? And, why did Susan initiate this meeting? Mary's assumption that the signs were Susan's doing would create a stormy interview at 'The Ranch'.

On the deck, Charlie stood at attention. His ears quivered as he heard the muscular sound of the Pontiac Firebird. As the newspaper reporter arrived, Susan headed out to the driveway to greet her guest.

Mary's curly red hair was tied into a bun and her hazel eyes were hidden behind oversized shades. She wore a matching grey skirt and jacket, white long sleeve blouse and high heels. Susan greeted her guest with an inviting, outstretched hand. "You must be Mary Wilson, I'm very glad to meet you. I'm Susan Schafer and this is my watchdog Charlie!"

"I'm honored to meet you, Susan. As you obviously have guessed, I'm here representing the *Riverside Gazette*. Hello Charlie. I promise to conduct myself professionally. I would hate to get on your bad side!" Charlie wagged his tail and licked her hand. It was shaping up to be a great day for Charlie! With Larry gone, Charlie would get the full attention of two beautiful specimens of the female, human kind.

Mary quickly sized up and mentally noted the splendor of the desert oasis. "Wow, you have quite a place here! Is that your Corvette?"

"That's my baby. Other than my husband, I don't have children to spoil, so I spoil myself."

Mary's assignment was to do a story on small town politics, a big time building moratorium and a council woman whose full time profession was a high school English teacher. Mary tried very hard to conceal her emotions, but she sensed that a teacher's salary would not support this kind of lifestyle. Mary Wilson entered this assignment intrigued. Now she was suspicious. The political arena had become her specialty. Unfortunately, many of her assignments ended up bringing out the worst in people, not the best. "So Susan, you must tell me the significance of the personal license plate."

"Those numbers represent the birthdate of John Lennon, October 9, 1940."

"Jumping bullfrogs! I bet that's an interesting story."

"Actually, it is. But I think you're here to talk to me about Lake Mathias and not John Lennon. So where did you get that bull frog exclamation?"

"A few years ago, my editor told me to clean up my act. I had a bad habit of using the expression, bull crap, so I re-trained myself to exclaim 'jumping bull frogs'. I don't even think about it anymore, it just pops out, but it's served me well. It's definitely a conversation starter! Anyway, Susan, the best stories I've written involve remarkable people, interesting places, and intriguing events. It's becoming apparent that all three of those elements will be in effect today! In two minutes, I've gotten peeks at signs, 'The Ranch', and John Lennon. By the way, I've lived in Riverside, a half hour's drive from here, my whole life. This is the first time I've ever been to Lake Mathias."

"Sounds like we have a whole bunch of ground to cover. Let me show you around a bit and then we'll grab a cup of coffee and talk. How much time do you have?"

"I've set aside all day for this. My editor is very eager to give Lake Mathias and the moratorium lots of coverage. And I'll be doing the covering!"

"I'm glad I got his interest. I called the *Gazette* on Monday, and here it is Tuesday and you're at my doorstep. The timing is perfect. The next Lake Mathias Town Council meeting is a week from tomorrow."

Charlie stretched his body into a position that would block the two beautiful women from the walkway that led to the house, assuring their attention once the driveway conversation was over.

Susan led Mary in Charlie's direction. "Must you lay right in the middle of the way?"

Charlie slowly got up. Both women patted his head and leaned down to accept Charlie kisses. Charlie had scored again!

As they walked towards the front door, Mary marveled at the inviting outdoor furniture. It was a crystal clear July morning. The view of distant Mount Baldy served as a towering contrast to the shimmering Lake below. Lake Mathias, from this deck, was small in size but spectacular in impact. Mary was overwhelmed.

"Mary, would you like to have our talk out here?"

"Yes, that would be great. It's a beautiful morning to enjoy the outdoors. Excuse me, but may I use your restroom?"

"Certainly, just proceed down the hall and you'll see it on the right. While you do that, I'll start a fresh pot of coffee."

Since Larry was in the plumbing business, the Schafers' bathrooms were comparable to those seen in a Home and Garden magazine. As

Mary walked into the bathroom, she was greeted by a stunning collection of amenities: a two passenger whirlpool tub and a designer pedestal sink with a toilet to match. The fixtures were trimmed with top-end antique brass faucets.

As Mary headed from the bathroom back towards the kitchen, she tried to remind herself that she shouldn't judge Susan by her Corvette lifestyle, even though she guessed the Schafers were on a Volkswagen budget. But, she was confident she would get to the bottom of everything. The process might not be as pretty as the view from the deck, but that really didn't matter. What mattered was the truth.

Larry and Susan had remodeled the kitchen themselves. The finished room became the centerpiece of 'The Ranch'. The panoramic view out the south window, proudly displayed the rattlesnake tree, the vast population of cactus, the gazebo, and the pool.

As Mary entered the kitchen, she gazed through the window to the south. "Your house is unbelievable. While we were chatting in the driveway, I didn't even notice the waterfall spa. I can certainly understand why you would be proud of the paradise you've created in this corner of the world. By the way, the bathroom is unbelievable!"

"The pool and spa were actually here when we bought the home, but they were a swampy green mess. The fixtures in the bathroom are Larry's doing. He has friends in the wholesale business who get stuck with special orders that are abandoned. Larry scoops them up piece by piece at ridiculous prices. We did all the plumbing installation ourselves."

Mary could only offer a one word response, "Stunning!"

"How do you drink your coffee, Mary?"

"Black, please!"

Susan's gut churned as she tried to read into the insinuations and body language of the reporter. Even though Mary was complimentary, she seemed overly polite, suspicious, and guarded. Susan followed Mary's lead, neither smiling nor frowning.

"Okay, Mary, shall we go outside to the deck and get started?"

As Mary and Susan walked outside, Susan continued, "Larry and I made the decision to buy this home because of this view. That decision was made before we even set foot into the house."

Charlie did not leave the side of the two women. Once they sat down, he picked a spot between them to plop himself.

Mary reached into her purse and pulled out a tape recorder.

"Mary, I love your Firebird. Is it a four-speed?"

"Oh yes, I love shifting gears!"

"Do you rev your motor with 'zwischengas'?"

"What?"

"Sorry! That's a Larry story!"

"Susan, before we start, I need to spend a couple of minutes on ethics and documentation. I'm now turning on my recorder. The *Gazette* requires me to ask you some questions."

Susan carefully measured Mary's comments about 'The Ranch'. She was always proud of her home, but Mary seemed to be making the complements like Nancy Drew uncovering a secret that would explain the unexplainable.

"Susan, here's the first important question. Are you aware that our conversation today will be recorded?"

"Yes, I am!"

"Do I have your permission to record our conversation today?"

"Yes, you do!"

"Okay, let's proceed!"

Mary sipped her black coffee. Susan was a little uncomfortable, but she hoped that it didn't show. This was the first time she had been interviewed by the media.

"Susan, here we are in Lake Mathias at your spectacular home you call 'The Ranch'. How long have you lived here?"

"About ten years. My husband, Larry, and I finished college and found careers nearby. This is the first and only house, we've owned. We purchased it as a 'fixer-upper'. Actually, it was a disaster! It had been on the market for over a year. Plus it was miles from anywhere and real close to being nowhere. Even at a distress sale price, there were no takers. So we put in a crazy low ball offer and amazingly it was accepted!

"Many of the renovation projects were done by us. I'm a teacher and have summers off. I spend most of the summer working on projects at 'The Ranch'. It makes me happy to dig in the dirt on a project and create beautiful surroundings. Larry is in the sales-end of the construction industry. He has contacts that cut us good deals on plumbing. He also knows lots of small contractors that have worked with us on larger projects, like the gazebo. When Larry gets a bonus for hitting a sales goal, we usually plow a good portion of it into improvements."

"I guess that makes sense. The result is truly amazing. Please tell me about the Lake Mathias town council."

"Members of the town council were elected by local voters. Because it's a non-paying position, it's always a struggle to find people willing to spend their precious spare time for public service. Historically, candidates get elected if they're on the ballot, as they are typically unopposed. There are four of us, plus Mayor Sam Calhoun, who is our chairman. Sam only votes on issues if his vote is required for a tie-breaker. Sam and I work closely together. Sometimes he drives me mad, but he is a good man who is good for the town. The other three councilmen are Rex Fisher, Blake Parker, and Jimmy Ray. I don't much care for Blake and Jimmy's politics! They're aligned with my husband's politics, on the right, just like Ronald Reagan. As for Rex, he's on the left side of the political aisle, but I really don't like or trust him!"

"Those meetings must be interesting. You're on a council with four men, and you don't like any of them!"

"Not true, when Sam is not driving me crazy, I adore him. As for Blake and Jimmy, they kind of remind me of Larry. When Larry is not driving me bonkers, I love him dearly."

"Let's talk about the moratorium. Where are you in the process?"

"We meet Wednesday afternoons. The disposition of the moratorium is coming to a head. The next meeting is on July 22nd and then in a town hall meeting on the 29th a decision will be made."

"So Susan, I followed your long trail of signs almost to your doorstep.

Your position on the moratorium appears to be well documented and blatantly obvious."

Susan's face turned bright, stop sign red. The signs were again tormenting her! "That is exactly why I called the *Gazette*. Those signs will be the death of me! And, I know you are recording this! You can keep that remark on the record! Those agonizing signs are not mine. That trail of signs was created by someone trying to influence my vote. I need you to help me find the money that's behind this. I really don't know how I'll vote. But the money behind these signs is making me want to vote against the notions the signs are promoting! And that isn't right either! Can you believe someone would build a trail of signs that leads to my home?"

Mary was stopped flat in her tracks. She had assumed that the signs were a campaign by Susan to influence the town into wanting the moratorium to die. She was ashamed of the things she was thinking. 'The Ranch'! The classic Corvette! The lifestyle! Mary's hunch that Susan was the recipient of money that influenced decisions for the council had just been proven wrong. Mary despised unethical behavior. She had authored many articles that exposed wrong doing. She now sensed that she desperately needed to re-set the table. "Susan, if you don't mind, I'd like to slip into Levis and tennis shoes."

Mary put the tape recorder on pause. Susan was not sure what had just happened, where she stood with Mary, or where this was headed. As she watched Mary walk down the path to her car, Susan reached down and patted Charlie on his head. A pat on the head always made Charlie feel good. In this case, the pat made both of them feel better.

Mary returned after a quick trip to her car and the restroom. She had literally let her hair down from her bun. The skirt had been replaced with comfortable jeans. The heels had been transformed into worn, comfy sneakers. When she first arrived at 'The Ranch', she feared that Susan would be exposed as another crooked politician. Now that had all changed. Her mood was transformed from procedural and stiff, to freewheeling and honest.

Susan looked with amazement at a perky Mary and was quick to re-establish her role as a hostess eager to please. "Well, that's a lot better; you look like you're relaxed now. All right, Mary, before we go back to work, let's refresh our day and our coffee."

"Let me give you a hand. This time, I'm thinking it's time to add a splash of milk to my coffee to make me smile and a sprinkle of sugar to make me sweet!"

"I like that! I'll have mine the same way!"

The two sweetened women returned to the patio. As Mary turned on the tape recorder, Susan sipped her coffee, took a deep breath and sighed, "Okay, Mary, let's see if that coffee sweetening business actually works."

The sips and the smiles broke the ice. In its place was the sweet sound of laughter. Mary turned on the recorder. "If there is any breach of ethics involved here, any idea where you would start looking?"

"Good question. I met a business friend of Larry's who is a contractor named Red. Red was very charming and quite clever. I rather like him! His advice was to follow the trail of signs to the money behind them. But I'm not sure what that means or how it would be accomplished. I'm hoping you will help me."

"I do like Red's advice. I think we first find out who owns the land that would be developed if the moratorium dies. The owners certainly have a special interest. With a little help from my friend who works for the county, I can get that information. Since there are property taxes on that land, it should be easy to get a list of the Lake Mathias property owners being taxed. Then it's just a matter of having it sorted from the largest to the smallest. My guess is that the top handful of names on the list will be very interesting. The next job will be to figure out if any of the council members have ties to the property owners with the most land."

"Okay, Mary Wilson, now you're talking like the Nancy Drew I was hoping for!"

"Jumping bullfrogs! Its 9:30! If I can use your phone, I'll call my friend now! If I can catch her, there's a chance she'll have the information ready before she goes to lunch. I can certainly proceed on my own, but if you're up for a road trip and an adventure, you can join me!"

Susan responded in a flash, "Count me in!"

Mary made her move to make the phone call when Susan stopped her. "Mary, I am so...so...sorry!"

"About what?"

Susan continued, "About almost everything. You jumped to a conclusion early on that I was part of the problem not the solution. And then I concluded that you were not capable of understanding the problem!"

Mary turned towards Susan with a puzzled look on her face. "I'll have to think about that. Is Larry capable of keeping up with your quick tongue?"

"Larry doesn't really understand me!"

"I think Larry and I have something in common. Let me make that phone call. We need to get the ball rolling!"

While Mary went into the house to use the phone, Susan sat motionless until Charlie got up and stuck his big brown head in her lap. After rubbing noses with him, she headed to the kitchen to refresh their coffees. Both cups were filled with sweeteners and smiles. Susan sat down and paused. Her mind was swirling like a Lake Mathias whirlwind.

Mary returned, "I talked to Sarah. I owe her lunch, but not today. She's working on the list as we speak!"

Mary took a sip of the hot coffee,."More sweeteners and more smiles. This is going to be a great story!"

Susan took a sip and responded, "Do you ever taste the bitterness of frowns in your coffee?"

"Only when I drink my coffee black!"

"That's how you started the day. Your first cup of coffee was black!"

"That's correct!"

"Until today, I always drank my coffee black."

"Well Susan, that explains just about everything!"

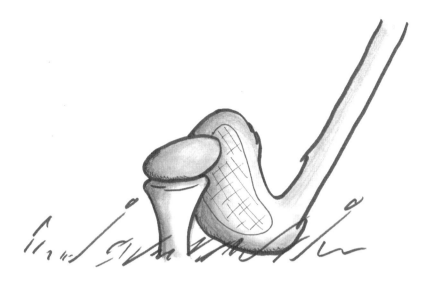

CHAPTER 11

"Sandbagging"

Papa taught Larry how to play golf. Papa was a golf enthusiast whose golf game did not match his enthusiasm, so the result was predictably bad. Larry's first golf shot in his life smacked a woman in the adjoining fairway right in the belly. Larry should have known, at that brief moment in time, that he and golf were incompatible. However, even though his skill set was short, his determination was as unrelenting as weeds in 'The Ranch' garden.

Over the years, Larry's golf game improved dramatically to a level precariously balanced between mediocre and awful. The thing he hated most about the game was that the harder he tried, the worse he got. It was opposite to any challenge he had ever tackled. So, he struggled.

Larry and Frank arrived at the golf course at 8:30. They had a 9:00 AM tee time, so on 'Frank time', they were actually ahead of schedule. They were playing Juniper Hills, their favorite course. The fact that Juniper

Hills was not a fancy country club suited Larry just fine. Given his golf game, flying way below the radar fit him to a tee.

Larry was an interesting dichotomy. He had a burning passion for the game, but he was horrible. Larry guessed he must love the game because he liked to be miserable.

Frank, on the other hand, played the game very well. In business, sales managers typically have a good game, and Frank was no exception. He spent the majority of his life on the road, in and out of hotels, packing and unpacking suitcases. It was a lonely existence. The trade-off was golf on the road trips with business associates. In short, Frank was a 12 handicap. Larry was a 30. The 18 stroke differential meant Frank would give Larry a stroke on every hole. This handicap would, theoretically, even the match.

Nancy was the queen of the snack shack. Her worn smile and tired eyes were consistent with a life-time of serving up hotdogs and beer. Although she survived on a minimum wage and pocket change tips, she was always pleasant and knew every customer by name. "Hi guys, any particular reason you've been avoiding me?"

Larry smiled at Nancy and replied, "Frank only lets me play once a month."

"Frank, you wouldn't fire Larry if he played a little more golf, would you?"

"Only if he started taking my money on the course!"

"Here's your coffee, boys. Have fun out there!"

The men walked into the adjoining pro shop to a smiling Dave McGee. Dave had waived good-bye to a career in a struggling carpet cleaning business. When boredom overcame him, and his wallet got light, he landed at Juniper Hills. The job got him out of the house, provided a little spending money, and included an important fringe benefit: free golf! Dave was able to negotiate a schedule that had him working Tuesday, Thursday and Saturday. That was perfect as his wife worked on Mondays and Wednesdays. On Sundays, Dave played golf at Juniper. It was hard to say who was happier about the schedule, Dave or his wife.

"Larry, I'm looking for a new teaching pro. I thought perhaps you would be my man!"

"Thanks, Dave. I would take you up on that, but it requires a rare skill set to swing a club the way I do. I'm pretty sure it would be impossible to teach."

"Larry, don't be taking too much of Frank's money. That's a damn good way to get fired!"

The men laughed and paid their green fees.

"Gentlemen, the course is wide open! Enjoy!"

The game of choice for Frank and Larry was a two dollar Nassau, a wager based on a hole by hole match-play competition. In this game, the total score for 18 holes of golf is immaterial. The objective is a net score (including handicap) on each hole that is less than the opponent's. It doesn't matter if the winner of a hole wins by one stroke or six strokes, it still counts as a single hole won. Whenever either player is two holes behind in the contest a new two dollar match called a 'press' automatically starts.

The golfer winning the most holes on the front nine wins two dollars and the winner of the back nine wins two dollars. Then, another two dollars goes to the player that wins the most holes overall.

The appetizer served before a match is a smorgasbord of posturing, dishing out, and receiving the most tired clichés the game has to offer. Amazingly, this mindless game is relished by every golf nut who ever bet with a friend on a golf game. And even more astonishing is that the participants go through the exercise as if it were a brand new experience. Since the air is filled with emotional outcries woven around spurts of ranting, and raving, an outsider would think the participants are playing for big money. Not so. In most cases, the wagers are for less than the cost of lunch.

"Larry, I hope you brought lots of cash. Your money will feel real good in my pocket!"

"I know, but as you know, I don't play golf every day like you do. I'm out there actually working! So how about you give me a couple of extra strokes?"

"Not a chance! I'm already giving you too many. I can't believe you expect me to give you a stroke a hole. That's highway robbery! Jesse James had a gun when he robbed people! The way you putt, you should be ashamed to take that many strokes!"

"That would be smart! You drive the ball 280 yards right down the middle. It takes me two shots to get to your drive. By the time I finally get to your ball, with the stroke you give me, we're even! See, I need the 18 strokes!"

"How about the short par 3's that only require a Larry-sized shot? You always kill me on those!"

"Exactly! But on the long par 5 holes you annihilate me! That makes us even!"

The pre-round conversation never varied. It was tradition.

As the men drove their golf cart to the first hole, Frank quizzed Larry, "How're you doing with Town and Country?"

Larry was closed mouth until a deal was really done, with order in hand! He knew that the best way for a salesman to look bad is to talk too much. He was well aware that bravado is fine on the golf course, but not in business. Too much conversation about his plan to secure Red's business would be embarrassing if his efforts were thwarted.

"As you'll remember Ernie is the buyer, and Ernie is an asshole. Since Red wants Ernie to do the buying, I'm doing an end around. Town and Country will be tough to get, but if we're really patient, there's an outside chance that one day we'll do some business. I'll keep you in the loop!"

"Not only are you a sandbagger on the golf course, you're a sandbagger on the job!"

The two men walked to the tee. The first hole was a par 4 that played 380 yards. A narrow tree lined fairway rewarded straight shots. "Okay, let me see what you've got!"

Larry's swing was neither athletic nor graceful. The most remarkable thing about it was that he could actually complete it without landing on his wallet. As body parts flew in different directions the impact of the swing on the ball was akin to a fourth of July firework that resulted in a dud.

"Good swing, Larry! I can't believe I'm giving you a stroke a hole! You're killing me!"

Frank's graceful swing was effortless. It was the kind of swing viewers watched on TV. As Frank's drive soared 150 yards past Larry, he mumbled, "Great shot, Frank. You have a really boring golf game, long and straight every single time! If I pay you now, can I discount the bill?"

"Not a chance. That would be far too easy. I want you to struggle and whine for 18 miserable holes, and then pay me!"

Frank's drive left him 90 yards to the green. His second shot with a pitching wedge carried high and straight but landed 30 feet short of the hole. Larry's second shot left him 80 yards from the green so he hit an eight iron for his third shot. The ball was heading into the direction of a sand trap, but it struck a rake and ricocheted towards the pin, stopping two feet from the hole.

"That's the luckiest shot I've ever seen! Don't tell me you're going to pull that crap on me!"

Larry walked up to his ball knowing that it was so close to the hole that it would be almost impossible to miss. "Is this good Frank?"

Larry also knew that Frank would not concede the putt to him, but asking for the concession, was another silly ritual that grown men, acting like children, play on the golf course. This game within a game is almost as fun as the game itself.

"Are you crazy? Mark that ball. We're putting them all in!"

Frank was first to putt. He rolled it straight and true. It looked like it surely would go in for a birdie, but stopped an inch short.

"You better mark it. I would give it to you if I could, but my boss taught me to putt everything in!"

Frank shook his head while Larry calmly rolled his putt in. Frank tapped in. Both men scored fours, but because Larry received a handicap adjustment his four was scored as a 3. He was one up!

"So Larry, I suppose you're going to tell me that pool shot ricocheting off the rake was by design?"

"Well, almost. By all rights, it should have gone in the hole!"

"God continually punishes me for rescuing you from Dick's Plumbing!"

The second hole was another par 4, but played straight up-hill. Larry hit low worm burners which are a liability anytime, but especially bad when playing uphill. Frank hit towering rockets that were unaffected by the grade of the terrain. Advantage Frank!

"So Frank, how are things going in the rest of your region?"

"Pretty damn good. I have some very powerful rep firms that are really getting great results. They have longtime relationships with wholesale distributors and contractors. For example, when we attack someone like Town and Country in Arizona, the rep there is already selling them other lines. That gives him a decided advantage. As a factory man you don't have that kind of leverage. That makes the job of converting business a lot tougher for you!"

"I thought Town and Country was easily the largest plumbing contractor in the west."

"Of course they are! That's exactly why I keep bugging you to get us that business!"

"Do your reps with the contacts have the same amount of expertise on our line as factory people?"

"No, but it's becoming apparent that their relationships more than make up for it!"

"It sounds like factory guys like me are going to get fired. I'll be sure to update my resume!"

"If you bounce another shot off a rake and land it by the hole, you will be fired!"

As expected, on number two Larry took an eight and Frank had a bogey five which evened the contest.

Number three was a short par 3 of 140 yards. Both men put it on the green and two putted. Larry's three netted a two with his stroke, so Larry was now one up. The par 5 that followed was an easy five for Frank. Larry took five shots just to reach the green and ended up with a seven. Again the match was tied.

"Damn it, Larry, you're making me work way too hard. Instead of playing golf every day, you should be getting 'Town and Country' on board!"

"You can tell from my Frank Caparelli swing that I play every day!"

"Where in the world did you learn that ugly swing?"

"From my Papa!"

"Who taught him?"

"He was self-taught. The technique is a hybrid!"

"Of what?"

"A ping pong volley and a fly swatter smack!"

After a gut busting laugh, Frank replied, "Since he drove the ball better than you, he obviously perfected that ugly swing!"

"His foot work was better than mine. He was a soccer player!"

Many putts had been made and missed since the passing of Papa and many bets had been won and lost since Frank, Larry, and Papa had played golf together. Frank remembered Papa's determination to keep his score correct. Since old age brought Papa forgetfulness, to ensure accuracy, he meticulously counted his strokes with a string of beads. Frank removed his cap and ran his fingers through his salt and pepper hair. "That Papa was one hell of a guy!"

The men ended up all square on the front side. The friendly opponents each won three holes and tied three holes. Larry shot a 54 and Frank...42.

"Seriously, Frank, do you think that $PROH_2O$ will ever move away from factory people in the L.A. market, and replace us with a rep firm?"

"There's actually been some discussion, but I think it's a ways off. You shouldn't worry! Worst case scenario, they would move you to the home office in Cleveland!"

"Cleveland is a long way from the beach! I want no part of that scenario!"

"Like I said, they're just chattering back there. For every move they actually make, they chatter about a hundred of them. I really wouldn't worry!"

"That's easy for you to say. You live out here in the sunshine and play golf year round. Any chance you would move to Cleveland to take a big corporate job so I can take your job out here?"

Frank looked at Larry as if he had just landed to Earth from Mars. "That sounds like a really great idea, Larry. You've either lost your mind or Nancy slipped a shot of Baileys into your coffee!"

"Okay, Frank! Okay, I know, I know!"

"You need to relax! You're trying to take my mind off the game so you can take my money! This will be an interesting back nine!"

"Maybe for you, but I feel like I just got fired!"

The tenth hole was a long uphill par 4. Frank easily won the hole. Number eleven was longer and more uphill. Frank scored a five, Larry scored an eight. Frank was now two holes up, which put a press into effect: a new bet from that point forward, plus the original wager.

Number twelve was a short par 4. If Larry hit two perfect shots, he could reach the green in two, which would put lots of pressure on Frank.

Larry hit his drive 160 yards, putting him in range to reach the green in regulation. That was a rarity. Frank hit a missile that left him a short chip to the hole. Larry's second shot was long enough but bounced into the right sand trap. A miraculous sand shot put him fifteen feet from the hole. Frank's chip put him two feet from the hole.

"Is this good, Larry?"

"Not bad!"

"Don't you know how to play 'boss' golf?"

"You taught me to never, ever play customer golf. I took that to mean boss golf as well!"

"You have an answer for everything!"

"Not really, this Cleveland business has me tongue-tied!"

Larry lined up his putt. If he made it, his score of four with his handicap stroke would make a three, meaning Frank would have no chance to tie or win the hole. It was a fast putt with a big break. Larry started the putt five feet right of the hole. As it built up speed, it broke sharply left and slammed into the hole!

Frank groaned. "If that ball doesn't hit the back of the cup and luckily go in, it rolls off the green and I win the hole!

"You can pick your ball up. We're now one and one."

Translation - Frank was one up in the match. Larry was one up in the press.

The two rivals tied the next five holes. So the match came down to a final par-3 hole requiring a 156 yard shot over a pond. Almost every man playing this hole would hit a mid-range iron for this shot, but Larry selected his driver. Even with the driver, he would need to strike it perfectly to get there. In this case, he didn't. The ball hit beyond the pond but the sloping turf kicked it back into the water.

A sarcastic Frank remarked, "That's a tough break, Larry. I thought you'd clear the water and land on the green. You know I was rooting for you!"

Larry scratched his square head and rolled his puzzled eyes. "I can see you're heartbroken!"

Frank hit a beautiful high trajectory shot that looked like it might be a hole in one, but it hit the flag stick and took a violent kick off the green landing just in front of the water.

"That should have been a hole-in one. You got robbed! The golf gods must want me to win!"

"You're killing me, Larry!"

"You know what Frank? Anybody could be a 12 handicap with your swing. I'd love to see you try to be a 12 handicapper with my swing. That would be a true test of your skills!"

"You are truly amazing! Where in the hell do you come up with this crap?"

Following the rules of golf, Larry took a drop, two club lengths away from the pond, a spot that ended near Frank's ball. The rivals were tenaciously playing for two dollars, not two million; but that was immaterial. The objective was to win!

Because of the penalty, Larry was hitting his third shot. He chipped his ball softly onto the green, but it hit the seam separating the green from the rough and rolled down the slope away from the hole. What should have been an easy two foot putt ended up twenty feet from the hole.

"Tough break, Larry!"

Frank hit a soft chip shot, rolling his ball a foot from the hole. "Can I pick this one up, Larry?"

"Absolutely not!"

"Can I mark my ball right here, or do I need to move it out of your line?"

"To be safe, you better re-mark one putter head to the right."

Larry struck his putt. It rolled and rolled and rolled…but stopped just short of the hole! Larry tapped in.

"That's a 5 for a 4, right?"

"Unfortunately!"

Frank placed his ball in front of his marker and was about to tap in for a 3 to beat Larry on the back nine, in the match and square the press when Larry stopped him, "You forgot to re-mark your putt to its original spot. You're lucky I stopped you before you hit that putt or it would have cost you a one stroke penalty!"

Frank sheepishly re-marked his ball and tapped it in. Frank had just beaten Larry out of two dollars for winning the back side of the match and another two dollars for winning the total. It was a hard fought win for four dollars. Were it not for Larry's good sportsmanship, the match would have been tied, and he would have won the press. In that case, Frank would have owed Larry two dollars.

The two men shook hands and embraced.

"Thanks for reminding me about re-marking my ball, Larry. That makes up for hitting the rake and beating me on number one!"

"I won't be able to pay my mortgage, but at least I'll sleep with a clear conscious. Here's your four dollars."

"As much as I'd like to, I just can't accept your money. You saved me a stroke on the last green. You could have easily let me proceed and then hit me with the penalty!"

"That's okay, you would have done the same for me. Don't embarrass me, take your four dollars. But don't spend it! I'm planning on winning it back the next time we play. Call me if anything is percolating in the home office about the company changing to a manufacturer's rep firm here! It scares the crap out of me!"

"I promise you, I won't let them send you to Cleveland! That would cost me anywhere from two to six dollars of golf winnings a month!"

"Yeah right, Frank!"

Frank reached into his pocket as he got in the last word, "Here Larry, have some jelly beans and quit your whining!"

CHAPTER 12

"Seaweed"

As Larry's Astro swirled up tornado dust clouds heading up Annie Oakley, his mind swung as wildly as his golf swing. From Red Starr to PROH$_2$O to the four dollars he lost to Frank and now to the signs. Those damn signs! Plus, there was the box. Not Susan's box, but a special box from Cleveland that would be delivered UPS.

As he looked ahead, there was another dust tornado. It was heading his way. The two tornados stopped in the middle of the road. Once the dust settled, both drivers rolled down their windows.

"We meet again! After spending the day with Susan, I feel like I know you. Remember me? Mary Wilson, with the *Riverside Gazette*."

"I sure do! Did you do more than stir up dust today?"

"Oh yes, I sweetened up your wife's coffee and then we made some very interesting discoveries."

"Is that good or bad?"

"It's definitely good. The end result is that Susan now has a sense of direction for how she'll deal with the council and the building moratorium. She has lots to ponder and resolve in her head, but now she's armed with the facts. As for me, it looks like my story on the moratorium will be on the front page!"

"What did you put in that coffee?"

"A splash of milk to make her smile and a sprinkle of sugar to make her sweet!"

"That's it? No Kahlua, no Baileys?"

"Oh no, to unravel the mystery of the signs, we needed to think clearly."

"You sound like Nancy Drew!"

"Jumping bullfrogs! That's exactly what Susan called me!"

Larry made an effort to size up the red head that seemed to be a combination of Nancy Drew and Mark Twain.

"If I get home, and Susan is that sweet, I might start using your bullfrog expression!"

Mary nodded and smiled. "It's been a pleasure meeting you!"

All Larry could do was scratch his square head and smile. "I'm looking forward to reading all about it in the *Gazette*. Perhaps then, it will all make sense."

Larry proceeded down Annie Oakley and turned up Penny Lane. Charlie was there to greet him. "Did you have a fun day with Susan and Mary, Charlie?"

Charlie wagged his tail, vigorously confirming Larry's speculation.

Larry entered the house as he always did, through the backdoor that led to the kitchen. As he walked in, he was greeted by one of Susan's favorite Beatle songs. After the day he had, he wasn't sure if he agreed, but the words 'we can work it out' kept repeating. Now he noticed a bottle of wine and appetizers on the counter, "Honey, I'm home!"

Susan entered the kitchen glowing and particularly stunning.

"You look scrumptious! Are we expecting company?"

"Nope, just you and me!"

"It's not our anniversary or our birthday, so what's the occasion?"

"I had coffee with Mary!"

"So I hear. I talked to Mary, briefly, a couple of minutes ago. That must have been some coffee!"

"So how was your golf day with Frank?"

"I lost four dollars and got fired!"

"You did not!" Susan was angry. Larry had a way of annoying her in record time.

"Okay, I left one part out. If we move to Cleveland, I won't get fired!"

"Cleveland, Ohio?"

"Yes!"

"Who in their right mind would want to leave California and move to Cleveland?"

"Exactly!"

Susan looked at Larry sideways, "Exactly what, Larry?"

"Well, not exactly."

"Not exactly what? Did you get fired or didn't you?"

"Well, no…"

"Well then, okay. That was an exhausting exercise! Did you or did you not lose four dollars to Frank?"

"I did."

"So, I guess that explains why you are so out of sorts!"

"I guess. Let's forget about all of that. Tell me about coffee with Mary."

Susan poured them each a glass of wine. "Boy, have I got a story for you. And mine even makes sense. Through Mary's help, we acquired a list of undeveloped property in Lake Mathias. And, we now know who owns it!"

Larry was now at full attention. "Really?"

"Oh yes. I have it right here."

"Let me see it!"

"Not yet, not until you guess who owns the vast majority of the property."

"I have to guess?"

"After what you just put me through, before you finally acknowledged that Frank beat you at golf again, yes, I'm going making you guess!"

"Okay, Red Starr!"

"Yeah, right Larry, no! I'm sure you can do better than that. Have a sip of wine. Perhaps that will sweeten your disposition and make you a better guesser."

"I'm sorry! It was a tough day on the golf course! I owe you an apology!"

Susan turned her head downward but towards Larry. Squinting eyes were replaced by a Mona Lisa smile. It was not the Susan look that froze Larry like a Popsicle when he said something stupid. This was a mischievous look, unlike any he had ever seen. After all these years, Susan had developed a new trick! Mary must have slipped something into that coffee! Perhaps it was not Baileys or Kahlua but instead Grand Marnier!

"Okay, Larry, let's hear a real guess!"

"Okay, Okay, but before I do, I need to ask you something before I forget. Did the UPS man deliver a box today?"

"Stop changing the subject! You've been acting very peculiar ever since you got home. One Bloody Mary makes your face turn tomato red, but makes you fun, not impossible. It's becoming clear that you and Frank had two. I'll answer your box question after you guess who owns the buildable land in town."

"Cedar Wood Developers?"

"Great guess! That's exactly what I would have guessed. The answer is no!"

Larry was surprised. Cedar Wood was Town and Country Plumbing's largest builder. Cedar Wood was the mastermind that promoted a sunny life in Sunnymeade by using the giant billboard signs that Larry and Susan passed on their way to the Flier's on Saturday.

"This is getting interesting! I'll make one more guess. What is the name of the realty company that Blake owns?"

"Great question. Maybe the Bloody Mary high you've been on is wearing out. Blake's company is called Hawkeye Realty."

"Okay, my guess is Hawkeye Realty."

"Great guess, but again you're dead wrong. You'll never, ever guess the answer!"

"Then why are you making me guess?"

If Charlie had a sign it would have been a yellow triangle that indicates, 'proceed with caution'.

Susan would have barked back, but that coffee had really sweetened her up. Instead, she took another sip of wine and sighed. 'The Workers Union.'

Susan had dropped out of the teacher's union over ten years ago, after serving one year as the school union representative. Even though she attended the meetings, she definitely did not drink the Kool Aid.

The union was vocal in its opinions and the representative's job was to make sure all members agreed with the union, regardless of their own beliefs. Susan felt the students were the losers in this proposition.

Her year as a representative culminated in a nasty, humiliating strike during which she actually walked a picket line. After the conflict was over she vowed to either quit the union or quit teaching. It was fortunate for the scores of students she taught, that she chose to keep teaching. She was the kind of teacher that made a difference; the kind of teacher that students respected and would remember for a lifetime.

Larry was amazed. "The Workers Union?"

"That's right! Explain that one to me!"

Larry's mind hastily gathered information before responding, "A union would probably own land for an investment that would benefit its members for the long term. Another motive might be to create jobs for union workers. Not that long ago, plumbing contractors like Town and Country were union. Red was one of the first major contractors in Southern California to form a non-union shop. I know you hate unions. Guess what, Red does too! If and when the union develops the land they own, they would require contractors on those jobs to be union, which would create jobs for their own people. Today thousands and thousands of workers are on a list at the union hall waiting for a union contractor to call them and put them to work!"

Now it was Susan's turn to be amazed, "My goodness, Larry, I didn't know any of that. Why have you kept that information a secret?"

"I was just waiting for the right moment to spring it on you! This is just that moment! So how does that affect the council and the moratorium?"

"Mary and I connected the dots. We connected the union dot to Rex Fisher, a big time union guy for the fire department!"

"You mean the Rex that is on the council?"

"That's the guy. I've never trusted him! I think he's behind the signs and is trying to 'fix' the vote."

"I thought you and Rex usually voted the same way?"

"That's true, but it's obvious his motives have been different than mine!"

"Now what?"

"We have our next council meeting a week from tomorrow. Mayor Sam will review the ethics that public council members must abide by. That will lead to some lively conversation. If I play my cards right, I'll suggest that, perhaps, Rex's union alignment and the union ownership of property in Lake Mathias makes for a conflict of interest. It'll be really interesting to see how that pans out. I know he doesn't like me!"

"Is it because you dropped out of the teachers union?"

"That may be a part of it, but not all of it."

Larry could not believe that Susan and Mary sorted all this out in a day. "I'd pay admission to watch this thing sort out. Susan vs. Rex! I really don't like Rex's chances of coming out of this thing alive! I thought Rex was retired. Are you sure he's still involved in the union?"

"My new friend Mary is like Nancy Drew. She can assemble pieces of a puzzle in nothing flat. She made a call to The Workers Union. Rex is part of the organization!"

"Hmmm, this is really interesting. Sounds like you followed Red's advice and followed the trail of money!"

"Larry, I really like Red. Give him a big hug for me!"

"If my plan works, I'm taking Red to Ventura on a road trip. I probably won't give him a hug, but I'll say 'Hi' for you. So what if Rex paints you as a union hater that has it out for the unions?"

"I'll tell the truth. I don't dislike unions. But, as you know, that strike absolutely turned me against the teacher's union. I will never forget how humiliated I felt holding up a protest sign. And to think I did that because I was told to, not because I wanted to, absolutely sickens my stomach. My quarrel with unions has to do with values not money. In this case it looks like there's a conflict of interest involving ethics and money!"

"Did you know that $PROH_2O$ faucets are manufactured by union factory workers?"

"Larry, I don't care a hoot about that. But, if those workers had a union man on the Lake Mathias board that tried to influence an important issue for this town because the union stood to benefit by the outcome, I would have a problem!"

"Perfect! Just make sure you keep that ammunition in your head when bullets start flying around you and Mayor Sam!"

"I'll be well armed. I've already filled in Sam. He and I are committed to having the council make a fair decision for the town. I aim to meet the truck half way, but if anybody tries to run me off the road, they'll be sorry!"

Susan's eyes were riveted on a Larry Schafer that sometimes made her crazy. But the battle of the signs and breakfast with Red at the Flier's seemed to bond them through some mysterious means. Suddenly, out of nowhere, they were actually becoming friends again. Their relationship in Ventura started as a friendship that developed into a love affair and culminated in a marriage now sixteen years old.

The lovers embraced. The hug felt like their first hug at Disneyland in the rain, thousands of arguments ago. They were about to kiss, when Susan flashed back to the beginnings of the evening's conversation.

"Larry, what's this business about Cleveland and $PROH_2O$. I want to know the part of the story you left out!"

"What makes you think I left something out?"

"Larry!"

"At the plumbing trade show last year, I introduced you to George Taylor, the owner of GT Sales. They are the largest rep firm in Southern California. They have contracts with key manufacturers in the industry. They sell water heaters, plastic pipe, sinks, toilets, copper tubing, and other products. Since their manufacturers pay them a commission, their sales volume dictates the income available to run their business. GT employs a powerful team of sales people and has an office to process the orders and service their customers."

"Well, what has that got to do with you?"

"PROH$_2$O is using sales agencies, like GT Sales, in other areas and, evidently, they're very pleased with the results."

"So they would replace you with GT Sales?"

"GT Sales or one of their many competitors. The move to rep firms sounds like it's being discussed. Frank said not to worry. He said it probably wouldn't happen, and if it did, I would be offered a job at headquarters in Cleveland."

Larry had only been to PROH$_2$O headquarters in Cleveland one time, and that was in the dead of winter after he was first hired. That was Larry's first and only experience with frigid cold and life inside the corporate bubble. He was sent to Cleveland to attend a class on professional selling. Since the class was scheduled to start Tuesday morning, Larry flew in on Monday.

Because the temperature was 78° when he left L.A., Larry dressed casually for the occasion, wearing polyester pants and a Hawaiian shirt. When he landed in Cleveland five hours later, the temperature was 18o°, a net loss of 60°.

After arriving to his hotel via an airport shuttle, Larry was welcomed to Cleveland. As he got out of the cab, his pants, shirt and body all froze into a giant ice cube. His first step onto frozen tundra sent him crashing to the ground on his tail bone. Larry was reminded of that fall every time he went to his chiropractor.

The driver helped Larry get up and collect himself. "Whoa there, big fella! Looks like you found some black ice! Welcome to Cleveland! Where are you from?"

"Los Angeles!"

"That explains why you're not wearing a wool coat, gloves and snow friendly shoes. What kind of outfit is that?"

"I like to dress just like the Beach Boys, but I forgot to pack a sweater!"

The driver rubbed his hands together to keep them warm. Larry had reinforced the driver's belief that California was the land of fruits and nuts. He wasn't sure if Larry was a fruit or a nut, but it didn't really matter. The driver offered the only remark that made sense at the time, "I don't think the Beach Boys ever come to Cleveland!"

Larry finally checked into the hotel, bought some winter clothing, and warmed his body with a bowl of hearty beef stew. A bloody Mary relaxed his mind a bit, but did nothing to help the pain in his back.

He was certainly not prepared for the brutal cold weather, but Larry was resilient. He recovered in time to make the sales class in the morning. The professional selling class taught the art of 'need-satisfaction selling'. A skilled, professional sales person with this skill-set asks a potential customer questions that reveal the customer's needs. He then satisfies the need by explaining the features and benefits of his product. More importantly, he explains how his product satisfies the need.

Larry learned how to sell when he was at Dick's Plumbing. Steve, the owner of Dick's, would make customers feel very important by asking smart questions about their needs. Once the needs were exposed, he offered solutions that would satisfy those needs. Writing the order was the logical outcome. Larry studied the technique and then patterned himself around it. Neither Steve nor Larry had any idea that this technique was 'need-satisfaction selling'.

So, Larry spent three days at the training class hobbling around in bitter cold weather learning a skill he already possessed. However, he did learn three things: First, beware of black ice; second, wool suits are popular in Cleveland for a good reason; and third, never live in a place where you can't be comfortable wearing a Hawaiian shirt.

The trip to Cleveland was the beginning of Larry's life with a bad back and the event that triggered the walk that inspired his nickname of Ratchet-Ass.

Susan nudged Larry from yet another daydream, "Larry, do you want to move to Cleveland?"

"People move from Cleveland to Southern California. Only a fool would move from here to Cleveland!"

"Thank God you said that! Now what?"

"My short term plan is sell Red PROH$_2$O faucets. My long term plan is to live here in Lake Mathias with you. The only way we are leaving Lake Mathias is a move back to Ventura. My head feels like it's full of tangled seaweed. Once I clear my head, I'll sort things out and develop a contingency plan to implement, if and when Frank calls me with news of a promotion to Cleveland. Looks like we both have lots of work to do. Where's that box the UPS man delivered? I'll need its contents to nail down Red's business."

As Susan handed Larry the box, a tear rolled down her cheek. Larry set the box on the counter next to the wine bottle. As they squeezed one another, their hearts became one. Larry's thoughts again took him back to Ventura. He recalled their walks along the beach. He remembered being so mesmerized by Susan that he absent-mindedly tripped on a maze of tangled seaweed that had washed ashore. Susan still had that effect on him. Her smile still made Larry's toes wiggle and his body temperature fire up like a boiler. But yet, they had their differences. Politically, they were donkeys and elephants. Susan would rather starve than eat a jelly bean. But all in all, Larry loved Susan because she was steadfastly loyal. When the seaweed of life got tangled inside his square head, Susan was always there for him.

Love once again triumphed over reality. Larry had been very eager to get a peek at the contents in the box, but Susan had swept that need aside.

As they walked down the hall towards the bedroom, their loyal friend Charlie followed faithfully behind. It seemed to Charlie that boxes had a way of creating drama at The Ranch. The next sound was a Charlie-sized whimper.

"It'll be okay, Charlie. Susan is going to outwit the Lake Mathias town council, and I'll make damn sure I outwit Cleveland, Ohio. Both of those things will be accomplished once we untangle the seaweed!"

CHAPTER 13

"High Pressure"

It was a sizzling hot Wednesday, July 22nd. The weather man said the 107o temperature was the result of a high pressure system. As Susan raced down Penny Lane, Larry mumbled to himself that the high pressure system in the atmosphere was no match for the high pressure system Susan would create at the council meeting!

Susan Schafer arrived at Lake Mathias High School at 2:45. The parking lot was empty and spooky quiet. Since it was summer vacation, she shouldn't have been surprised. But reality was far from her mind. She was like the theatrical performer who prepares for a big production of Hamlet, only to discover that there is no audience.

In Susan's case, no audience was scheduled to be there, but a supercharged spirit sometimes neglects the most blatant examples of common sense. While Susan was busy dress-rehearsing in her Corvette, she was joined by Kathleen Katz, the school secretary who would be taking the 'minutes' of the council meeting. She drove an orange 1961 Chevrolet Corvair, an auto that Time Magazine would later list as one of the 50 worst cars ever manufactured. Kathleen would have agreed. She was always on the look-out for a sale on motor oil, which she kept in ample supply in the front trunk of the rear engine convertible. She also kept a tool kit and a supply of serpentine fan belts in the car. The Corvair was a triple threat: leaking oil, burning oil, and shredding engine belts ridiculously configured into a figure eight pattern.

Susan watched as the Corvair's screaming six-cylinder engine sputtered to a stop in the parking spot next to her, a trail of oil marked the road as far as the eye could see. "Hi Kathleen, looks like you're leaking some oil."

"I swear I'm going to paint this car lemon yellow and then torch the whole damn thing. I would sell it, but I just don't have the stomach to stick someone else with it!"

As Susan looked up, she saw Blake Parker, Jimmy Ray, and Rex Fisher all pull into the lot as if they were on a car rally. Blake arrived in his 1986 white Dodge Caravan. Magnetic signs on both sides advertised his real estate firm, 'Hawkeye Realty...Homegrown in Lake Mathias'. The Caravan was the trendy alternative to big clunky luxury cars or station wagons. Senior citizens and physically challenged people liked it because it was easy to get into and out of. Blake liked it because it had big windows for house hunters he was working with.

Jimmy Ray pulled into a spot next to Blake and honked the horn of his working man's truck, a white 1984 GMC with big tires and rims. Jimmy's personal license plate read GR8HM4U. His license plate frame read "Custom Homes" on the top and "BY JIMMY RAY" on the bottom.

Rex Fisher trailed behind in his brand new black Cadillac that still had temporary license plates. It was a show stopper that attracted Susan's attention in the time it takes to quickly jump to a conclusion. Susan turned to Kathleen. "Somehow it just doesn't make sense for a retired fireman to be driving that car!"

The four council members shook hands with each other and with Kathleen. They would again be meeting in the library, which was directly across the parking lot. As the group practiced the art of small talk, the sun beat down on them with the fury of hell's revenge.

"Damn it's hot," quipped Blake.

"On days like this, my customers add swimming pools to their contract with me," replied Jimmy.

Susan could not help but comment, "Well, that certainly makes a lot more sense than driving a black car that soaks up the heat on a sizzling hot Lake Mathias day."

Susan's comment stopped all four of the council members in their tracks. Rex replied with his standard line, "Firemen love it hot!"

Heads turned as Mayor Sam pulled into the lot driving his 1953 Chevrolet, a car built like a tank and ready for warfare. Sam bought it for $60 in 1967. He had been the proud owner for twenty years. A classic car for the price of three dollars a year was an indisputable bargain. Every part of Sam's car was original, including Sam. The bubble shaped roof was dark green. The balance of the car was sea green trimmed generously with chrome. Sam had recently repainted it to the original specifications, but added air conditioning for heat waves like the one now in play. The chassis sat the height of Jimmy Ray's truck and the seats stood tall and firm. The steering wheel was gigantically oversized and the dome-like roof provided headroom that would suit Wilt Chamberlin. Because Sam stood five foot eight inches, he didn't just slip behind the wheel, he climbed.

When he drove that Chevy around town, he was both king and mayor. A six-cylinder engine generated the pedestrian horsepower and a three speed manual transmission, with the shifter on the column, was a blast to drive, but not appropriate for 'zwischengas', which is most effective with a robust motor. Like the mayor himself, the '53 Chevy was a distinguished, workmanlike, plodder. Chevrolet would later build robust re-designs of the '53 and '54 models. The 1955, '56 and '57 models became sexy, powerful instant classics. Not so for the '53. But Sam was more than happy with that because both he and his '53 Chevy were content traveling in life's slow lane.

After he parked, Sam grabbed his briefcase and duck-waddled his way to catch up with the group. By the time he got there, sweat was dripping off his bald head. But as usual, the mayor was unruffled. His trademark, red suspenders kept his pants up, but Susan believed that perhaps the suspenders also supported his disposition.

"Hello ladies and gentlemen. It's a beautiful day to be alive, even in the midst of a heat wave."

Once the group made their way off of the parking lot asphalt and onto the tree-lined sidewalk, the heat wave was forgotten and the business at hand took center stage. The moratorium! What to do with the moratorium?

Sam took the lead, unlocked the door and led the group in. The library was sizzling. Jimmy quickly flipped the thermostat to activate the air conditioning. The cooling unit made lots of noise, but the output of cool air was minimal. They all took their seats at a round table that allowed everyone to speak and be easily heard. Kathleen went to the refrigerator in the back and returned with plastic cups and a pitcher of ice water.

Sam started the meeting. "Dedicated members of the town council of Lake Mathias, thank you for serving this wonderful community. I will again remind you of the town charter which calls for the mayor to vote only if needed for a tie-breaker. We are gathered here today to discuss the expiration of the moratorium on housing that has been in effect for the past four years. There has been a great deal of publicity on this matter. The *Riverside Gazette* has publicized our moratorium challenge. It seems that a reporter named Mary Wilson has taken an interest in our small town. I understand that she has contacted each of you and has referred to specific conversations she has had with you. I've also made note of a sign campaign aimed at letting the moratorium die."

Susan, her emotions overflowing from the 'High Pressure', interrupted Sam's opening remarks, "Does anyone else have a trail of signs that leads right up to their house? Mary Wilson was under the impression that they were my doing, which is absolutely untrue!"

The rest of the council shook their heads no.

Susan continued, "I find it disturbing that I've been singled out for this sign bombardment. It's either making it look like I've taken a stand to kill the moratorium or it's trying to persuade me to vote that way!"

The mayor interrupted Susan's interruption, "Thank you very much, Mrs. Schafer, but if you're quite finished, I would like to continue!"

Susan sighed and quietly steamed as Mayor Sam continued, "Since the moratorium will be voted on in our town hall meeting exactly one week from today, it's of the utmost importance that we review and discuss the code of ethics to which we are bound. Each of us was provided copies of this document when we were elected by our fellow citizens. For your reference and convenience, I've brought copies of the twelve tenets to which this council is bound."

Sam passed out copies of the provisions adopted by the town of Lake Mathias six years earlier, in 1981. The council members carefully read through the tenets before the mayor continued, "Do any of you have questions?

Blake stepped right up. "In regards to tenet number four, I must ask, if by being a realtor, I should step down from the council. In the long run, the death of the moratorium would probably increase my opportunities to sell a house, which of course would benefit me."

Jimmy Ray added, "I guess I'm in the same boat as Blake. I build custom homes, not tracts, but I guess if the moratorium was not renewed, I would potentially benefit if more folks started taking interest in moving to Lake Mathias and building a custom home."

Tenet number four was creating quite a fuss. Sam took control. "Alright folks, this is exactly the kind of discussion I was hoping that we would have. Let's read this 'sticky' tenet four out loud together."

"Elected officials shall not have involvement, influence an outcome or vote for or against any provision that could potentially benefit them or an organization they belong to or are affiliated with, beyond the general benefit of the provision to the whole of the community."

While the group sat in silence, Kathleen continued to take the minutes of the meeting. She sensed the critical nature of the dialogue, feverishly noting everything!

Susan took a drink of water as the group sat in a paralyzed silence. She glanced at Rex who was fidgeting, but didn't utter a single word.

Mayor Sam maintained control and continued, "Blake and Jimmy, I really appreciate you fellows speaking up. As you all know, I am neither judge nor attorney. I am a simple man who spent a lifetime educating children. However, from where I sit, neither one of you two are in violation of this tenet. It would be impossible to have a council member that by and large would not have some sort of direct or indirect ax to grind. In your cases, there is certainly not any tangible, direct link that would make a citizen in this town think that something was up. On top of that, everyone in town knows what each of you fellows do for a living. And if they ever forget, they will be reminded by the signage you have on your vehicles. I believe this tenet has more to do with a public servant who has a direct benefit which fattens his wallet or the bank account of the organization he represents. For example, let's say I owned a big chunk of the buildable land in town. If I then voted to end the moratorium, that would represent a direct conflict of interest; at least in my mind. Ultimately, it will be the people who decide. As you all know, in this great country of ours, any citizen that suspects wrongdoing can file a complaint, and with the assistance of an attorney, litigate the matter. Again, I must remind you this is just Sam Calhoun speaking his own opinions."

Susan took command, "Mr. Mayor and distinguished fellow members of the Lake Mathias town council, if I may, I would like to suggest a course of action!"

Jimmy Ray, Blake, Rex, and Sam all looked up at Susan as if she had just put on Mayor Sam's suspenders. Never, ever had Susan been this formal, diplomatic, or political. This was a new Susan. Where was she going with this?

"As the mayor said so eloquently, it is not for us to decide what is right or what is wrong. Our decision on the moratorium should be in harmony with the will of the town. Our citizens should have an opportunity to decide what is in the best interest of Lake Mathias, and just as importantly, what is not. I suggest that each of us contact Mary Wilson of the *Riverside Gazette* and disclose any potential conflicts of interest as defined by tenet four. We should also request that the Gazette list all twelve tenets so that they can be reviewed by our citizens. If our fellow citizens object to any of us because of a violation of tenet number four, or for that matter, any of the twelve tenets, let them bring it up at the town hall meeting."

Rex could no longer hold his tongue, "Susan, you're turning this whole damn thing into a witch hunt! Talk about opening up Pandora's Box! This thing is likely to turn into a nightmare! I won't stand for it or be part of it! Our personal stuff is personal, and is nobody's damn business!"

"My, oh my Rex! You sound like a man who has something to hide. I wonder if it has anything to do with The Workers Union owning most of the buildable land in town. Oh, and may I add, that you are on The Workers Union payroll? Was it you or the union that planted a trail of signs that led directly to my house? Let's hear it! Is it getting hot in the kitchen, Rex? You did say that firemen like it hot!"

After what seemed an eternity of silence, Rex got up from the table, stormed through the library, and slammed the door. Moments later his black Cadillac disappeared into the heat of a burning Lake Mathias afternoon sun.

Mayor Sam had lost control of the meeting to Susan. The unflappable Mayor Sam was suddenly rattled. The high pressure system in the atmosphere had now settled into the Lake Mathias library. "Let's take a ten minute break and then devise a plan that will get us out of the hot pot of stew that Susan just dropped us into."

During the break, Susan talked to Jimmy and Blake. She repeated what Sam had said. She saw no conflict of interest in their circumstances. Their personal life might slant them one direction, but the same could be said of Susan and Sam, who loved the small town feel of a town with a little over 5,000 people spread around a fairly large area. Susan talked to Sam and told him that the council should consider meeting the truck half way. The previous moratorium called for building not to exceed 26 houses a year on lots not less than two and a half acres. Since the passage of the moratorium four years earlier, the maximum 26 permits were issued by the end of January each year.

Sam brought the group back together. "Okay folks, let's get back to work!"

The temperature of the library started to cool down. It was unclear if it was because the air conditioner kicked-in, or because Rex Fisher left the room.

The mayor casually re-set the table. "Well, Susan, it sure looks like you're making things lively."

Susan sighed. "Mayor, it's been a busy week. I need to fill you all in on the events that shaped this meeting. Mayor, you mentioned Mary Wilson. My nickname for her is Nancy Drew. She's the one that found out about the union owning so much of the land here in town. She also confirmed that even though he is retired from firefighting, Rex is still involved in The Workers Union. Mary will be reporting her findings in tomorrow's *Gazette*."

Susan now addressed Blake and Jimmy, "Gentlemen, I would follow the mayor's advice and call Mary. She will figure stuff out anyway, so you may as well be proactive and call her. As for the moratorium, we have attacked the issue of the 26 house moratorium as a 'yes' or 'no' proposition. I would like to offer a third potential solution. It seems a bit crazy to kill the moratorium and let builders build willy-nilly like they are in Sunnymeade. On the other hand, a 26 house moratorium is rather limiting. So I'm suggesting that we consider choices of A, B and C."

Susan had the attention of the group in the palm of her hand.

Sam interjected, "So what is option 'C'?"

"Option 'C' would be to allow the construction of 125 houses: 50 on one acre parcels, 25 on two and a half acre parcels, 25 on 5 acre parcels and up to 25 on 10 acre parcels. This would be coupled with a provision requiring builders to pay our town fees of 5% of the appraised value. Our council would disperse these funds for parks, ball fields, equestrian trails, school initiatives, etc. This would raise the quality of life for everyone! Option 'C' would be our way of meeting the truck halfway!"

Mayor Sam smiled and shook his head just like Larry shakes his head when Susan is on a roll. "That's all quite interesting. Perhaps you should be the mayor and I will retire!"

Susan shook her head as if to say 'no'. "With all due respect Mr. Mayor, it's only because of your leadership that we on the council can voice proactive solutions that are good for the town!"

Even Kathleen laughed at Susan's response. "Would it be proper to include emotions like laughter in the minutes of this meeting?"

The group laughed again.

Sam continued, "Susan, the way to pursue the third option you discussed would be to bring a motion to the floor. It would then need to be 'seconded' and then put up for vote. Would you like to proceed accordingly?"

"Thank you, mayor! Yes, I would!"

Susan repeated her proposal. Kathleen asked if anyone wanted to second the motion, which Jimmy Ray affirmed. Kathleen put the measure up for vote and it passed unanimously. The mayor supported the proposal by pulling on his suspenders and smiling contently.

He added closure, "Let's see if we can all get this straight. For the moment there are now three council members remaining. If Rex stays on the council, there will be four. In either event, given three voting options, there is a possibility that the mayor will cast the deciding vote!"

Sam's old eyes twinkled as he asked Susan, "So this truck that you're suggesting be met halfway, where's it from and where's it going?"

Again, laughter!

"Let's adjourn and move this meeting to Sal's for an ice cold lemonade. All in favor say, 'Aye'".

Three enthusiastic 'Ayes' nearly shook books from the upper shelves of the library.

After tidying and locking up, Mayor Sam Calhoun, Blake Parker, Jimmy

Ray, Kathleen Katz, and Susan Schafer all headed for the big parking lot expecting to see five lonely cars. Susan looked up to see a surprise sixth car: a royal blue Firebird with chrome wheels. She immediately recognized it as Mary's, "Hi! What brings you to Lake Mathias on this hot Wednesday evening?"

As usual, Mary was perky and ready. "Jumping bullfrogs, Susan, I thought perhaps you'd invite me to Sal's."

Susan introduced Mary to the group. Sam was quick to encourage Mary to join them, "It'll be our pleasure for you to join us! By the way, how did you know we were going to Sal's?"

"Susan calls me Nancy Drew!"

Kathleen replied sarcastically, "Just follow the trail of oil from my Corvair! That'll lead you to Sal's!"

The caravan of cars arrived at Sal's at 6 PM. Six cars added to the two that were already there, filled the parking lot. Sal greeted the group as they entered and seated themselves at their customary round table in the back. He reserved the table for Wednesday council meetings. He always liked to find out the inside scoop. "So what's it gonna be on the moratorium? Will it be a big yes or a big no? And by the way, what did you do, replace Rex with this redhead?"

Susan was still driving the show. "Okay, Sal, here's the deal. Make sure you write all of this down. It's very, very important! We all want lemonade. We might not be voting yes or no but instead voting to meet the truck halfway. Rex is recovering from a high pressure system in the library and Mary is the redheaded reporter who is doing an article about Sal's Café and the council meeting for the *Riverside Gazette*!"

CHAPTER 14

"Cards"

The Astro was freshly washed, and the gas tank was full. Larry made sure it was loaded with PROH$_2$O samples and literature. In preparation for the big day with Red, he not only negotiated special pricing for Town and Country, he engineered programs for service parts, model homes, and a rebate with the factory. Plus, the kicker, the mystery sample box not even Frank knew about. Larry checked, double checked, and triple checked the list. He was ready!

As Larry drove down the expressway and passed the Flier's Café, he retraced the good fortune that had blessed him on his quest to sell PROH$_2$O faucets to Town and Country Plumbing. Four weeks earlier, he met Chip and Candy at the Flier's and discovered that Red ate breakfast at the Flier's early every morning. As Larry passed a giant billboard he was reminded of the hands-on, jobsite breakthrough with Chip and Charlie at the Golden Horizons job.

After turning right on the second road just past the split rail fence, Larry recalled how 'Frank Time' had saved him and the unforgettable lump in his throat when he discovered that Ernie had agreed to a meeting with Larry that he had absolutely no intention of attending. But good fortune found Larry again when he met Red in the lobby. He remembered being impressed by Red's easy way and, of course, his belt buckle. Based on early impressions, striking a deal with Red, and not Ernie, became his mission.

At the fork in the road, Larry veered right and passed one barn, and then another. As he did, his mind took him back to breakfast at the Flier's with Red and Charlie, and then again with Susan and Red. Neither Larry nor Susan would ever forget Red's suggestion to meet the truck halfway.

The broken down tractor on the right had given up all hope. If only that tractor had the gritty determination that Larry possessed, it would be turning over the soil for new crops to be planted, grown, and harvested.

Since the arrangement was for Larry to pick up Red at 7 AM for a road trip to Ventura, he arrived at Town and Country at 6:40. Frank would be proud. Since this would be a road trip and not a typical sales call, Larry wore his favorite outfit: Levis, a pocket T-shirt, and tennis shoes. He left every bit of his sales ammunition in the van, with the exception of four packets of business cards, each rubber banded separately.

He walked through the huge, wood grained double doors of Town and Country Plumbing with a quiet, unwavering confidence. As was the case when he and Frank had an appointment, the early morning arrival guaranteed there would be no receptionist to direct traffic.

The shop was an amazing example of organized confusion. Red's plumbers were methodically gathering, mapping, directing, smoking, or sipping their black coffee. When all else failed, they yanked the bill of their Town and Country caps or scratched the contagious itches that lodged between the pockets on the rear of their jeans or smack between the two front pockets, just below the zipper.

In the midst of the chaos, came a friendly yell from across the room, "Hey, Larry!"

Larry turned, scooted across the lobby, and slapped Chip's extended hand for a celebratory high-five. "Did you have French Toast at the Flier's?"

"Of course! Have you met our buyer, Ernie Nelson?"

"No, I don't believe I have."

A reluctant hand shake between Larry and Ernie followed.

"Ernie, Larry's the faucet guy I told you about. You should be buying his faucets. He really has his shit together!"

Ernie grumbled, "How is it that you know Chip, but you haven't called on me? Evidently you don't know who does the purchasing around here!"

Larry was undeterred, "Actually, I do know you are the buyer. Red has made that quite clear!"

Larry turned to his right, as a smiling Red reached out to shake his hand. "Hello, there Ratchet-Ass. Looks like you're getting acquainted with Ernie!"

"I certainly am. If I was here to sell something, I'd be talking to Ernie!" Larry unbundled one of his packets, handing one to each of the men. "Here's my card!"

Led by Red and Chip, roaring laughter followed!

DOG TRAINING BY RATCHET-ASS

YOU BRING'EM...

I'LL TRAIN'EM

791-SMRTDOG

Once again, Ernie was odd man out, and all because of this square headed faucet salesman. Ernie was on the outside of an inside joke which was cause for great embarrassment. His laser eyes attempted to burn a hole thru Larry's card. When that failed, he ripped it up and stuffed it into Larry's T-shirt pocket.

Chip interrupted the awkward moment, "Holy shit, Larry, now I know why you brought Charlie to the Flier's. You're a faucet salesman and a dog trainer!"

The only thing that kept Ernie standing in the lobby was Red: the man he loved and respected. And, most importantly, the man who signed his paycheck.

Red acknowledged the steam blowing out of his buyer's boiler-like head and attempted to be the peacemaker, "Ernie, this is just a bunch of good old boys having a little fun. Don't be getting all worked up about nothing!"

Ernie mumbled to himself, "The next time I see that Ratchet, I'll run his ass through the jaws of my 'peddler shredder'!"

The 'peddler shredder' was Ernie's office. He had an oversized desk fit for the plumbing king he thought he was. A file cabinet on each side, framed the barren desk that was not cluttered by even a solitary piece of paper. His executive chair sat high, as if on a pedestal. Across from his desk were two puny, uncomfortable chairs that paled in the shadow of Ernie's throne.

He loved to harass salesmen who called on him. A sign above his desk challenged the philosophy of a humorist and beloved American icon, who was famous for saying that he never met a man he didn't like.

"WILL ROGERS NEVER MET ERNIE NELSON!"

Ernie's desk was outfitted with minimal accessories. A pen and pencil set, a business card holder, a note pad, and a sign that was displayed in the center and angled directly at any visitor:

"PLEASURE. EVERYONE GIVES IT.
SOME BY ENTERING A ROOM, SOME BY LEAVING IT!"

He had been in the business a long, long time, perhaps too long. He didn't appreciate Larry's childish sense of humor, and he certainly didn't appreciate being embarrassed in front of his boss.

Larry handed Ernie his PROH$_2$O business card. "Anytime you want to talk about faucets, call me or page me and I'll be more than happy to swing by to see you. Please remember, it's a bit challenging to have a meeting when only one of us shows up! It's like expecting a poker game, but ends up being a game of solitaire!"

Red motioned to Larry. "Okay, Ratchet, that's enough; it's time for that road trip you promised me!"

Ernie turned and steamed back to his office. Chip veered over to report to the foreman of his job. Larry and Red headed out of the office to explore Ventura. Perhaps in Ventura there would be fewer growling old dogs like Ernie, and maybe Red could find a place by the sea where an old cowboy would be welcome. Larry was intent on teaching an old dog new tricks!

CHAPTER 15

"Pitch at the Beach"

Compared with the turmoil at Town and Country Plumbing, the Astro was a sanctuary. As they headed west, Larry looked into his rear view mirror. Dust clouds of dirt stirred up by bulldozers in Sunnymeade, were a faded sun-drenched haze in the distance.

"So, Ratchet, how's my girl Mrs. Ratchet doing?"

"She got home late last night from the town council meeting feeling like Muhammad Ali after he punched out Joe Frazier!"

"Wow!"

"By the way, she really likes you. She asked me to give you a hug for her."

"Thanks for offering, but if you give me a hug, I'll make sure that ratchet works its way a little tighter in your ass. So what happened in the meeting?"

"You won't believe it!"

Larry turned off the last exit in Riverside, pulled into a gas station, and returned with a copy of Thursday's *Riverside Gazette*.

"Here you go, Red. Looks like Susan's friend, Mary Wilson, gave Susan top billing!"

The headline read...

"SMALL TOWN POLITICS BECOMES BIG TIME CONTROVERSY"

"So Larry, give me the inside scoop."

"Susan decided to take your advice. First off, she and her friend from the *Gazette* followed the trail of money. It ended up at the steps of The Workers Union Hall."

"Those sons-of-bitches. I'm so damn glad I'm a non-union shop!"

"A guy named Rex Fisher is on the council. Turns out he works for the union and the union owns large chunks of buildable land in Lake Mathias!"

"Very interesting!"

"Because of his conflict of interest, the mayor expects Rex to resign today!"

Red kept pumping Larry for more information, "So where does that leave Susan?"

"Susan made a proposal to the council to meet the truck half way!"

"That's my girl. How will she do that?"

"Until yesterday, the council was voting a flat yes or no on the moratorium. Susan proposed a third option that the council agreed to consider. The third option provides for a substantial increase in the permits the town will issue in return for building fees. The town would issue up to 125 permits divided into groups of 1, 2½, 5 and 10 acre parcels."

"That's smart. Less cookie-cutter and she's meeting the truck half way! Sounds like I should buy some acreage in Lake Mathias for a new ranch!"

"Great idea, but it'll cost you a little more! There'll be a 5% fee that goes to the town for projects that will theoretically improve the quality of life. You can't build unless you pay!"

"Larry, I'm afraid to say this is entirely my fault. I hate it when people take my advice, run with it, and in the end, it costs me money. Son-of-a-bitch, she IS meeting the truck half way. How about those signs that are tormenting her?"

"Mary from the *Gazette*, whom Susan calls Nancy Drew, traced the signs back to Rex through a printer in Riverside. They believe that Rex's plan was to put pressure on Susan to vote for killing the moratorium. That would allow Rex to actually vote for keeping it. He would do that because the moratorium would be killed without his vote. That way, if anybody dug up stuff on his tie to the union, he'd look like a good guy."

As the conversation flowed, they were making good time on the interstate. They were now in the heart of Los Angeles, about an hour from Ventura.

"Larry, pull over. I need to pee, and I need a cup of coffee!"

Larry pulled into a gas station. He still had half a tank, but since he had the opportunity, he filled up anyway. Red returned with a cowboy like grin and cups of coffee for both of them. "Here you go Ratchet. I also got us some jelly beans."

"So, you did listen to me ramble about the *Jelly Beans in Life?*"

"Regrettably, I need to say, yes. Plus, your favorite president eats them on TV when he's giving a speech!"

"Have you ever noticed that jelly beans are a turd softener?"

"What?"

"Yeah, you share your jelly beans with a turd like Ernie, and before you know it, the turd is softened!"

Off and running, they went onto the Ventura freeway.

"You and I need to sit down with Ernie next week. I want to get you guys pulling on the same end of the rope. Make sure you bring those turd softeners!"

"That would be great! Thank you!"

As Larry drove, he took on the role of a tour guide, pointing out the general direction of Cal State Northridge. "That's where I graduated from college!"

"Aren't we a long way from Ventura?"

"It took me exactly one hour and ten minutes to drive from Ventura to CSUN in my VW. I transferred to CSUN after spending two years at Ventura College. I was able to work out a schedule where I took a full load of classes on Tuesdays and Thursdays, and then worked Monday, Wednesday, Friday and Saturday at Dick's Plumbing. The governor of California signed my diploma on July 23, 1973."

"Who was that?"

"Ronald Reagan!"

Red rolled his eyes, "I should have figured that. What was your major?"

"English!"

"English?"

"Yes, English!"

"Do they teach the art of creating confusing conversations in English classes?"

Larry smiled. "I did enjoy the creative part of the curriculum."

"I agree with the creative part, but, as you've witnessed, I use different adjectives to describe your creativity. Son-of-a-bitch! Dog Trainer! I love that card! Turd softener! You must have a truck full of creative shit in your head to come up with this stuff. I really, really need to keep a close eye on you. You're full of smelly, tricky shit!"

Red continued while Larry drove. "I told you that we're not interested in switching faucet suppliers. But, if we were, what kind of deal are you talking about? As you know, the bidding is competitive out there. I can't afford to pay extra money for all the goodies that Chip told me about!"

"I understand! I would never ask you to look at something that would hurt you. You should only make a change if you're absolutely positive that it'll be a change for the good! Changing faucet lines is a real big deal!"

Red nodded as Larry continued, "Now I need to ask you a ten dollar question. What do you like about your program with Alpha, and what don't you like?"

"Damn it! Here you go again! You give me a ten dollar question that turns out to be a twenty dollar question! Hmmm. Well, the prices are good. I don't think you can beat my Alpha pricing. And they give me a nice rebate that really helps my bottom line. So, all of that is good. What don't I like? Let me think. Well, missing parts are always a struggle. But I can't believe your factory workers are any smarter than Alpha's. On the other hand, you and I both know that Alpha's roman tub valve installation is a problem! Chip is your best salesman. He showed me a sample of your valve. It's pretty slick!"

"I don't suppose you'd tell me what your rebate is, would you?"

"Come on, Larry! How smart would that be? Plus, it wouldn't show much loyalty if I sold Alpha down the river after all these years."

"Okay, I respect that. Who's your Alpha go-to-guy?"

"I don't talk to salesmen, only dog trainers! You need to ask Ernie that question!"

"By my calculations, you buy about 84,000 faucets a year. It seems to me, that it'd be smart for you to have a relationship with a three million dollar factory!"

"Well, your math is probably right, but I don't need to know these people. All I need is for Ernie to be happy with them!"

"Sorry, Red, I thought you signed the checks, not Ernie!"

Red squirmed and fidgeted. That damn Ratchet-Ass was getting under his red freckled skin. It pained Red to hear Larry bring up a sore spot that Red knew to be the truth! But that still didn't make the medicine go down without Red spitting it back up!

"Damn you, Larry! Why in the hell are you always so damn difficult? You're becoming a ratchet in my ass!"

Larry opened his window. There was a cool ocean breeze in the air. It was well over 100° at home and 65° in Ventura. Larry and Red had just picked up 35° of comfort.

"How do you like the smell of the salt air?"

Red looked at Larry. He was so damn easy to hate and then in a fraction of a second, so damn easy to like. "Oh yes, I love it!"

Larry exited the 101 freeway at Seaward Avenue.

Red was impressed with the small town feel of Ventura. "Where in the hell is everyone?"

"This is Ventura, a small town that happens to have a beach. There aren't many movie stars here. You might find a few old cowboys hanging around, but not many movie stars. Johnny Cash's first love lives here. I delivered a water heater to her house! Don't you agree that Johnny Cash is an old cowboy?"

"I guess so. Doesn't your cowboy president have a ranch somewhere up here?"

"Just north of here, in Montecito. I think he's at his ranch, the Western White House, this week mending fences, riding his horse, and developing a strategy to corral Gorbachev. And, don't forget, President Reagan is the cowboy with the white hat!"

"Oh boy, there you go again. So you're trying to sell me on Ventura because two of the most famous cowboys in the world have connections here?"

"You are a cowboy, aren't you?" Larry reached into a third bundle of cards and handed one to Red.

RATCHET-ASS REALTY

NEXT TO JOHNNY'S BEACH BUNGALOW

UNCROWDED VENTURA, CALIFORNIA

ASK LARRY FOR THE COWBOY SPECIAL

Red laughed so hard that his face turned the color of his name. "Ratchet! You are stinking killing me, but don't forget that Johnny Cash wore a black hat!"

"Okay, Okay, but kick those boots off! Let's take a walk on the beach! By the time we get back, Johnny's Beach Bungalow will be open and we can have lunch. I'll show you where Susan's mini skirt shrunk to her waist and almost gave John Lennon a heart attack!"

"Did they teach you the art of bullshit in English 101?"

"It probably goes back further, but English classes sure shaped my creative thinking. Growing up, my brother, Otto, always told me to act normal; any idea why he would say that?"

"Beats the hell out of me, Ratchet!"

As the tide moves out, it deposits tangled mazes of kelp. "Ratchet, don't get your big clumsy feet tangled in that seaweed!"

"Okay, but inside my head, I'm untangling seaweed as we're walking!"

"Why in the hell do I feel like I need an interpreter to translate your bullshit?"

"What bullshit?"

"The seaweed bullshit!"

CHAPTER 16

"Meeting the Truck Halfway"

Larry had a gut feeling that $PROH_2O$ would make the decision to replace him with a rep agency. If $PROH_2O$ were to have a shake-up, it would be announced in July. That timeline would assure the reorganization would be in place on August 1st, the start of the next fiscal year. If $PROH_2O$ pulled the trigger, Larry wanted to be ready. The source of the tangled seaweed in his head was the business plan that would be his road map for starting his own rep sales agency. He had written a business plan, but there was still some work to do and some things to figure out. Cash flow projections were his biggest challenges.

As the two friends walked along the lonely shore, the waves relaxed the mood. This was Pierpont Beach, not Malibu or Newport. The Ventura beach community was connected by a series of parallel lanes that all ended at the sand. Beach bungalows and a few two story homes lined the narrow, alley-like, lanes. Prestigious ocean-front estates stood at the end of each lane.

The men turned their heads to admire a newly remodeled beachfront property with an open seaside deck and a 'For Sale' sign. "What's the cowboy special on that place?"

"I think you'll come out pretty good with a trade-in!"

"Trade in my old farm house for beachfront property? I like it here, but we're a long way from the shop!"

"I'm not talking about trading in your farm house. I'm talking about trading in your faucet line. I'm hoping to save you enough money that you can buy that beach house with the difference. You can use it for a get-away. When the temperature is hot, builders are on your ass, and the thought of only half of your men working gets under your skin, you can come up here to Ventura and relax."

"So that's the cowboy special?"

"That's the cowboy special for a special cowboy!"

"Ratchet, you're so full of that seaweed bullshit I can't even believe it. You must have smelled the shit you are full of when you picked plumbing as a career. So, tell me about these hot prices you're quoting me!"

"It's from the distributors currently supplying you Alpha faucets. You'll find our pricing within a couple of pennies of your current pricing. On some items I'll be a little high. On others, I'll be a little low."

"That won't buy me much of a beach house!"

"Who determines the brand of faucets that goes into the houses you plumb?"

"In Orange County, the builder calls the shot but in the Inland Empire, where I operate, I do!"

"Does Alpha give you no-charge product for your models?"

"Hell no, are you telling me that you would?"

"We're not offering free models to any of your competitors. But because of your volume, we can justify free models for Town and Country. We know as a fact, that Alpha is providing free faucets for models to large contractors, like you, in other areas of the country. I'm not aware of them doing that here, but they're definitely doing it elsewhere!"

"We'd give you a list of model home product and you'd ship it to my shop, no charge?"

"Yes. We would also pay you labor to change out your builders' existing model home faucets!"

"Okay, Ratchet, now we're getting somewhere. How about those parts that are a ratchet in my ass?"

"I would set up a supply of spare parts in each of your job trailers. As a service to you, I would personally refill them as needed, free of charge. I would also provide on the job training for your finish men. I would teach them how to install our product the most efficient way possible. I'll prove to you that you'll save labor and headaches by switching to our product!"

"You train dogs and plumbers?"

Larry smiled as Red continued, "I'll need to think about it. Sounds like you don't have a rebate."

"I didn't say that! You might be different, but Alpha is offering contractors you are competing with a dollar for every faucet purchased."

Red shook his head in agreement.

"We would propose a program predicated on volume. It's a step ladder rebate that starts at one dollar but increases as your volume with us goes up. The top tier is $2.50 per faucet. Based on your current volume, you would easily be able to reach that tier. And that's on top of the model home program!"

Red took off his cowboy hat and ran his fat fingers through his thin hair. Larry hesitated, but kept right on going. This was no time to stop his pitch. "To assure you of the quality of our product, we would fly you to beautiful downtown Cleveland, Ohio, and take you through our factory and engineering lab, but not in the dead of winter. If you want to go in the winter time, you're on your own!"

"Larry, I think you've misrepresented something here, and it may be a deal breaker!"

"What?"

"First you told me you're a dog trainer. Then you told me you're a realtor. I have the business cards to prove my accusations. It looks to me like you're just a damn faucet salesman trying to teach an old cowboy some new roping tricks!"

"Okay, Red, you've got me there. Let's head over to Johnny's Beach Bungalow and grab some lunch. Follow me!"

Larry took Red in the direction of the Pierpont Lanes. They walked down Hanover Lane as the sun broke through the morning fog. In just a few steps, blue sky broke through. The two friends turned left towards Seaward Avenue, and minutes later they were back to the van, slipping on their footwear. As Larry grabbed his sample from the back seat and pulled his proposal from his brief case, his pager beeped. It was Frank. The two men walked into Johnny's and found a booth in the corner. A big open window easily accepted the ocean breeze.

"What're you having, Red?"

"I don't drink on company time, so I'm having a root beer."

"I'll follow your lead. Please order our drinks. I need to make a quick phone call. My boss, Frank, is looking for me and he only beeps me if there's something important brewing!"

Larry walked to the back of Johnny's and made a credit card call to Frank.

"Larry! Thanks for calling me back so quickly. I would normally want to deliver this news in person, but I'm in Montana. I've got good news and bad news."

"Holy crap!"

"Listen to me Larry! Listen carefully! The bad news is that the company has made a decision to go with a manufacturer's rep firm to cover Southern California!"

"I've been afraid of that!"

"Wait a minute, Larry! The good news is that we're offering you a new position as our sales trainer. We all agree that you're the most skilled salesman we have! The company has really big plans for you!"

"I know I'm reading between the lines, but it kind of sounds like a piece of shit topped with whipped cream and a cherry!"

"Larry, settle down! For one thing, you'll be getting a promotion and a healthy raise!"

"So what's the other thing, Frank?"

"Well, Larry, it means you're moving to Cleveland!"

Larry had rehearsed the untangling of this seaweed in his head over and over again, so he responded quickly with confidence, "Here's my deal in a nutshell. Number one, I'm not moving to Cleveland. Number two, as soon as I get back to my table at Johnny's Beach Bungalow in Ventura, I'm closing the deal with Town and Country. Number three, you need to hire me to be your new rep. I'll have my agency in place by the time you get back from Montana. If $PROH_2O$ doesn't want to make me the rep, you guys can kiss Town and Country's business good-bye!"

"Damn, Larry! You really have a way with words. Let me digest all that crap! Call me at my hotel here in Montana tomorrow morning at seven. It's the number on your pager!"

Larry hung up the phone and took a deep breath. His hands were shaking. His head felt like it would explode. He stood motionless, trying desperately to steady himself. After finally regaining his composure, he re-joined Red.

"Okay, Ratchet, from the look on your face either Frank just kicked your ass or you just kicked Frank's ass!"

"I think it was both!"

The two men looked at the menu.

"What's good here, Larry?"

"The salt air, the kick-back feel, and the fish and chips are on the top of my list!"

The waitress with tight jean shorts and a bikini top came to the table.

"Ratchet, I want you to meet Amy. Amy, this is Ratchet."

Amy smiled and turned to Larry. "I'm so sorry, what did you say your name is?"

"Larry!"

"Okay, fine, the crashing of those darn waves must be affecting my hearing. I thought Red, said your name is Ratchet."

Red took charge, "Larry is a ratchet, but that's a long, long story, and we'll be here at the beach a short, short time. Amy, this will be an easy order. On top of the root beers we're both drinking, we're both going with the fish and chips!"

"Perfect. I'll be back in a flash with some more root beer!"

Larry recalled that sixteen years earlier, he and Susan were drinking root beer when Susan stopped John Lennon in his tracks. The more he thought about it, the more it seemed like there was a trail of Jelly Beans connecting 1972 to 1987.

Red got the conversation back on track, "Are you gonna show me what you've got in that folder and in that box, or are you gonna tell me about your conversation with Frank?"

"Actually, both! I'm going to give you this folder and everything inside of it! Let me just go through it real quick!"

Larry reviewed the parts program, the model home program, the rebate program, and the distributor quotation.

"Damn, Larry! That's one hell of a program, and you even put it in writing!"

Larry opened the box and pulled out a sample of a single lever kitchen faucet and handed it to Red.

Red grabbed the faucet sample. In his hands was the best Christmas present he had ever been given, and it wasn't even Christmas! The faucet handle was in the shape of Red's belt buckle. The letters RS were forged inside a star and the star was formed into the rectangular buckle handle. It matched Red's belt buckle exactly!

Red was not easily impressed, but his emotional old eyes beamed as if they were transmitting a message from his cowboy heart. Larry Schafer had just shaken the boots right off of Red Starr's feet.

Larry continued, "The pricing and program would be based on this custom belt buckle handle on the kitchen faucet. Other faucets would have our standard handle."

"Damn it, Ratchet, you're damn hard to say no to! I can't believe you made a faucet that exactly matches my buckle. But I'm not sure I would want every homeowner in Sunnymeade owning a copy of it. But it would be nice to have this sample in my farmhouse and my Ventura beach house. As for switching all my faucet business to you, I've made a decision! I love the cowboy special!"

Red reached over and shook Larry's hand. The shake was both firm and genuine. It was the kind of shake that only occurs when business partners bridge the gap separating business and friendship.

"Red, do you remember that last line in the movie 'Casa Blanca'?"

"Ratchet, this is the beginning of a beautiful relationship!"

"Exactly!"

Amy's timing was perfect. "Here you go boys. Fresh from the sea and onto your plates; enjoy your fish and chips!"

The men celebrated their partnership and gobbled up the greasiest, most mouthwatering fish and chips this side of New England.

"Ratchet, when you and Mrs. Ratchet come up here and stay with me in my beach house, we're coming back to Johnny's!"

Larry told Red the story about Susan's mini skirt and John Lennon.

"Looks like Johnny's Beach House Bungalow is a good luck charm. I've been trying to get the work of Inland Builders for seven years. I think I'll bring them up here for some fish and chips. I've tried everything else. Maybe that will do the trick!"

Larry scratched his head. He was not sure how to tell Red about his conversation with Frank. "So, Red, it's about time we head home. On the way back, I'll tell you all about that phone call!"

Larry looked around the table to see if Amy had left the check.

"I know you're looking for the bill, Ratchet. I've got it. My treat!"

"Thanks!"

"Ratchet, this is the beginning of this old cowboy building a relationship with his three million dollar faucet rep."

After Larry's pitch at the beach, they were back on the 101 and on their way home. Red was still clutching the RS belt buckle faucet as if he had just won first place at the county fair.

"Red, I know Ernie is your buyer, and he talks to salesmen. But are you friends with any manufacturer's reps like GT Sales?"

"I wouldn't say they're my friends, but I kind of know all the big reps and even some of the smaller ones. There are only a couple factory sales guys, like you, that call on us."

"Frank just told me that PROH$_2$O is going from factory sales people to reps in this market."

"Crap! Where does that leave you?"

"I've been offered a promotion, if I move to Cleveland!"

"What did you tell him?"

"I told Frank that I wasn't moving to Cleveland, you and I just made a deal, and if they didn't want to screw up our deal, they should make me their new manufacturer's rep. When I get home I'm faxing Frank my business plan. He told me that there was a chance this might happen, so I've been busy putting together a contingency plan. By the time I call Frank tomorrow at 7:00, my proposal should be well digested."

"Sounds like you're going into business!"

"I know Frank pretty well. I'd bet you ten bags of jelly beans that I'll be PROH$_2$O's new manufacturer's rep!"

"If you need some help, I can loan you some money to get started!"

Larry was overwhelmed. First he overwhelmed Red. Now Red overwhelmed him!

"That's amazingly generous, but your support in buying PROH$_2$O faucets will be all that I'll need!"

"So, Mr. Ratchet, what are you calling your new company, Jelly Bean Sales?"

Larry laughed and reached into the center console to grab the fourth bundle of business cards. "I'm pleased and honored to make you the first recipient of my new business card!"

"That was one hell of a speech. Sounds like they really do teach the art of bullshit in English classes!"

Red spread out the four different business cards Larry had given him, and kept grinning from one red ear to the other. He looked back at the custom faucet Larry had somehow engineered. Then, he thought about his father, the man who had designed and crafted the one-of-a-kind buckle that Red cherished; the buckle that reminded him of Rodney Starr, who was not only his father, but his hero and best friend. Red looked back at Larry's cards and smiled again. He now focused on the card he had just received.

Connection Sales

1151 Penny Lane

Lake Mathias, Ca.

Pager: 791-RATCHET

"Connection Sales?"

"Yes! In business it's paramount to connect dots. Unconnected dots amount to disappointed customers and lost business opportunities. Connection Sales will aim to connect all the dots!"

Red gave Larry a north-south head shake. "That may be the first thing you've said all day that makes any sense at all. If you're really able to connect those dots, Larry, you'll definitely be less screwed up than your competitors."

"Okay, Red, now that I'm in the rep business, I'm going to ask you to meet the truck halfway."

"What in the hell are you talking about? The truck has been loaded and shipped. We have a deal!"

"I'm not talking about that truck; I'm talking about the next truck. Let's say I become the rep for a water heater company, would you meet that truck halfway?"

"Damn you, Ratchet! You're stinking killing me. Yes, I'll meet you halfway on any truck you send my way. Just don't send me a truckload of unconnected dots or seaweed bullshit! So, what brand water heaters are you talking about?"

CHAPTER 17

"Rattlesnake Tree"

L arry always drank his coffee black. Ever since she met Mary, Susan added a splash of milk to make her smile and a sprinkle of sugar to make her sweet. Larry had not recognized Susan's new sweetness, but that was understandable. He was a man. Rex certainly did not detect any sweetness when Susan uncovered his divisive sign campaign and scored a technical knockout over him at the council meeting.

Larry's life and his future were as foggy as a Ventura morning. It was hard to say if he was untangling the seaweed or the seaweed was strangling his precariously balanced square head. Charlie had already been fed, but was always on the prowl for any tidbits that fell from the counter to the floor. He sniffed every inch, but found no sign of seaweed. For that matter, there was not a drop of milk, a tasty crumb, or a granule of sugar to be found either.

When Frank accepted Larry's proposal and PROH$_2$O put Larry and his newly formed company, 'Connection Sales', into business, they benefited by keeping Larry on the team. He was a star salesman who knew the ins and outs of the key Southern California market and had just secured Town and Country Plumbing's business. Plus, he knew their products and the faucet business top to bottom. PROH$_2$O would also benefit by reducing their fixed costs. The commission based incentive that manufacturer's reps worked on is easily budgeted for and removes a host of variables.

If Connection Sales succeeded and even thrived, it would be because Larry did it his way. His vision was to create a business environment that would be bold, impeccably honest, and undeniably fun. That's how Ronald Reagan did it. And that's how Larry Schafer would do it!

Forefront in his business plan was to do such a great job with PROH$_2$O, that Connection Sales would attract other manufacturers of plumbing related products. Once that occurred, the Jelly Beans in Larry's life would be as vibrant as the candy colors and as sweet as Mary and Susan's coffee.

Larry had already secured a small office next to Sal's and hired Candy, the Flier's waitress, to be his office manager. He also made offers to two of PROH$_2$O's Los Angeles salespeople who were casualties of the company shake up.

In order to minimize the start-up costs, Larry's plan was to bring aboard the salesmen September 1st, which meant that during the first month he would be doing the work of three plus overseeing the office and training Candy.

Susan poured steaming hot coffee into the John Lennon cup Larry had given her for her 30th birthday. Larry's favorite mug was a 50 year PROH$_2$O commemorative edition. As Susan filled it, she noticed a blank look in Larry's eyes. Clutching her Lennon cup, she suggested a change in venue, "Let's drink our coffee up in the gazebo!"

"What's wrong with the kitchen?"

"Charlie needs the exercise!"

As Larry, Susan, and Charlie hiked to the gazebo, the morning sun shone through the citrus trees that marked the eastern boundary of

'The Ranch'. It was a warm peaceful morning. Susan was sure that the gazebo was the perfect place to slow down a day that had the makings of becoming a crossroads in their lives. To be sure, recent events in a crazy month of July were re-routing Larry and Susan's life onto a rocky untraveled road.

As they walked up the winding path, they were greeted by an Easter Lilly displaying magnificent petals that would be here today, and tragically, gone tomorrow. Charlie led the way. His trail walking ritual of moving ahead, lifting his leg, and circling back was in harmony with the swing of his tail.

Larry's mind swirled back to Ventura. There was a magic in Ventura that Larry could not explain. He and Susan met, fell in love, and started a life together in Ventura. Larry and Red were in Ventura when Larry closed the deal with Town and Country. And in a life-changing phone call at Johnny's Beach Bungalow in Ventura, Larry boldly told Frank that he was not moving to Cleveland. That last daring ploy put Larry into the manufacturer's rep business!

And here he was in Lake Mathias married to Susan, doing business with the largest plumbing contractor in the country, and doing something that in Ventura he vowed never to do. He was starting a business in the business of plumbing. Big Ben's words still echoed in his ear, "Plumbing is something that will help you the rest of your life!"

In spite of what Larry's Ventura College business professor preached, Larry rarely wore a tie, and today was no different. Business casual was Larry's standard operating dress code. He wore a sports coat when he called on builders, mechanical engineers, or architects. Jeans and tennis shoes were the norm for job-site visits. He did dress for success, but he did it his way!

As they sat down, with Charlie at their feet, Susan sipped her sweetened coffee. "Larry, I'm scared!"

"Is it the thought of being married to a business owner that scares you or are you worried about Rex making a counter-attack at the meeting tonight?"

"Both! What if your income projections are wrong and you don't have the money to pay for the office or your employees? What if you can't pay us? What if we can't make our mortgage payment and we lose 'The Ranch'?"

Larry was also scared. He was venturing into a universe of unknowns. There were no guarantees in business. His contract with $PROH_2O$ could be terminated in 30 days. Connection Sales would not be officially starting for four days, but Larry was quietly playing the same 'what-if' game that Susan was playing. As he sat on top of the world, in the gazebo, sniffing the aroma of coffee from Brazil, he felt a knot-like tightness in his chest that would not go away.

Was he having a heart attack or was it anxiety? Would it ever go away or was this the punishing tax that the body assesses on the mind for taking on a risky venture?

Larry pushed his secret fears aside and made a play to reassure Susan,. "Everything will be just fine. Frank was able to convince management to loan Connection Sales enough money to get us through the first ninety days. Business should be ramping up and getting better every day! As you know, Red is converting all his business to us! A 100% conversion will take about six months. Once we get that business, we'll be in great shape!"

"But we've always lived within our means. Other than the house payment, we've never borrowed money for anything. I don't think I like the idea of you going into business. Teaching may not have the financial up side of a successful business, but on the other hand, it's steady and reliable. It certainly beats the heck out of a bad business!"

"I thought we agreed that we didn't want to move to Cleveland?"

"You're right, you're right. I'm just scared. But what if your jelly bean eating president's plan to trickle down money from the top never reaches the bottom, or even the middle, where we are?"

"The president believes in the private sector. He wants to provide people like you and me the opportunity to live the American dream!"

"I can't believe you're buying into that nonsense!"

"In honor of the president, I was thinking about handing out a bag of jelly beans along with my business card. What do you think?"

"Oh boy, now I'm really getting worried about this new venture of yours. I suppose you'll have jelly bean promotions to drum-up business?"

"That's a great idea! I can't believe I didn't think of that!"

"I wasn't being serious. Customers would give you an order to receive a bag of jelly beans? I don't think so, Larry!"

"Jelly beans would be frosting on the cake! I really like your idea! Good thinking!"

"As usual, you're not listening to me!"

"Really?"

"And tell me something! Why in the world would you hire a waitress to run your office? Of all the dumb things you've done, that may be the dumbest one yet!"

"Candy has something that can't be taught!"

"A great figure and a sexy walk?"

"I'm not talking about that Susan. Candy just knows how to make people happy!"

"Is this a plumbing business or a brothel?"

"That is absolutely uncalled for. Candy has a business degree and is completing her Master's program at UCR?"

"If she's so darn bright, why is she working at the Flier's?"

"Well, I'm happy to say that she just smartened up. She now works for me!"

"Larry, by going to work for Connection Sales, she didn't smarten up; she just dumbed down!"

Charlie got up and started heading back down the trail. He stopped, turned around, and barked, as if to tell his masters that the verbal ping pong game was over and it was time to go home. The Schafers took Charlie's lead. The trail was blazed on a bed of granite that made the down-hill hike a bit treacherous. Larry was always happy when he made it to the bottom without landing on the tailbone he injured when he slipped and fell on black ice in Cleveland.

As they took deep breaths from the ping pong and the slippery trail, Larry and Susan reached flat land. They turned down the path that led them around the rattlesnake tree, near the swimming pool.

Larry looked up to see why Charlie was barking. That was a mistake! He should have been looking down. A rattlesnake was sunning himself and coiled in the middle of the trail. When Larry stepped on him, the jaws of the startled diamondback rattler's jaws tore a hole right through his slacks and drew blood in his upper thigh.

"Damn!" Larry screamed the same way he did when he was bucked off his donkey and landed head first onto a gravel road. Charlie watched the rattler slither through the crack of a big rock. His whining bark was directed at both the rattler and the rattlesnake tree.

Susan was shaken, but very much in control. "Pull your pants down!"

Larry was in shock and stood motionless. Susan unbuckled his belt and pulled his pants down for him. She grabbed a towel from a lounge chair, dipped it into the chlorinated water of the swimming pool and gently wiped the wound.

"AHHHH!"

"Sorry! That will sterilize it a bit!"

"Are you going to suck out the venom?"

"You've been watching way too many movies. Let's get you into the car and to the hospital."

Susan jumped behind the wheel of the Astro for the first time in her life.

"Okay, you square box of bolts. Show me see what you've got!"

As they raced down Penny Lane, Charlie barked in machine gun staccato, as if to sound a signal for the whole town. Susan kept control and gave Larry instructions, "Hold that wet towel against the wound!"

Larry followed Susan's instructions. The white towel quickly turned into various shades of red. It was a twenty minute ride to the hospital, but Susan made it in less than fifteen. As they sat in the overflowing emergency room, Susan smiled lovingly. "Looks like we might be here a while!"

Larry replied sarcastically, "So this is the real definition of being snake bit?"

Susan laughed. Even in an emergency room in distress, Larry made her laugh. "You'll be just fine! If we're in here too long, I'll call Mayor Sam and move the council meeting here to the hospital!"

As they laughed, a nurse called Larry's name and led them through the security door and into an exam room. The next thing Larry could remember was lying on a gurney in a worn and stark hospital room with Susan at his side. The doctor came in for a post operation review. "Mr. Schafer, rattlesnake bites don't usually kill people, but they can!"

"So I'm screwed?"

"Not at all! To the contrary! We detected no venom in your system!"

"How's that possible?"

"It's hard to say, but it probably has to do with a combination of things. Your wife did you a big favor by wiping the wound with chlorinated water and getting you here quickly. Hopefully that will prevent an infection. As for the venom, it may have been released before the snake's jaws bit into your leg. The other plausible explanation is that the snake's attack was a dry strike. Dry snake bites, with no release of venom, occur about 25% of the time. On top of that good fortune, you were lucky that the snake bite was not a fraction of an inch higher. A genital wound would not have been fun for either one of us!"

Larry heaved a sigh that filled the room. "Now what?"

"You need to keep fresh bandages on the stitched up wound, take the prescribed antibiotics, and take it easy!"

"I'm not good at taking it easy!"

"Your body will tell you when you're pushing too hard. We are all unique!"

"Doctor, you don't know Larry like I do. He is uniquely unique!"

"That became obvious when we stitched him up!"

The seaweed in Larry's head tangled a bit more as the doctor and nurse both wished Larry and Susan well. The clock had jumped forward to 2 PM. The town council meeting was at 5 PM, so there was no time to waste.

As they headed down the road, the fog in Larry's head began to lift and the seaweed loosened the stranglehold it had on his thinking. "So you were in the operating room when they stitched me up?"

"I certainly was!"

"Larry, as I saw you laying on the bed, I was reminded of how much I love you. You're undoubtedly one of a kind, but I think perhaps that's why you are so dear to me. But Larry, I need to ask you a question. It seems to me that I'm number four in your loves. Now that you've hired Candy, I may have slipped to number five. I really think that when we lived in Ventura, I was your number one. What happened?"

"What? I have no idea what you're talking about! I've never, ever cheated on you!"

"That's not what I'm talking about Larry. Never mind, I'm hungry!"

"I don't know why, but loving you is exhausting! There's a McBurgers on the corner!"

Susan navigated the Astro through the drive thru. The only casualty was the side mirror that hit the stucco wall as the van turned towards the window.

"This truck is just way too big! You won't see me driving this thing again!"

"Good!"

As Susan turned out of the restaurant to head back to 'The Ranch', Larry sorted through the bag. "Do you want the French fries or the burger? We only received one of each!"

Susan suggested a compromise, "Let's meet the truck halfway. Let's split both. Which side of the burger do you want, the first half or the second?"

Larry handed Susan the hamburger. "Since you saved my life, I'll let you eat the first half!"

"Larry Shafer, that's one of the nicest things you've ever done! Thank you!"

"I'm trying to show you that you're not number five! Do you believe it now?"

"Larry, please continue to be nice until I tell you to stop. You just tied your previous record for being nice to me!"

"You mean to tell me that you keep track of that as well?"

"Yes, one was the record, and you just tied it!"

Susan ate her half of the hamburger and passed it to Larry. Since women were the biggest mystery in Larry's life, he stared at the burger in hopes that the secret to understanding women would be revealed somewhere between the mustard and the pickle. After staring at it for an eternal moment, he determined that the answers must be hidden elsewhere!

CHAPTER 18

"Jelly Beans in Life"

The much anticipated Lake Mathias Town Hall Meeting was just two precious hours from becoming reality. That meeting would not only reveal the fate of the housing moratorium in a sleepy town, but would also measure the political clout of one Susan Schafer, a tenth grade English teacher. This big time controversy could very well determine the political future of a John Lennon loving, Corvette driving, Democrat married to a jelly bean eating, Republican businessman with a square head and a ratchet ass.

Life is miles of seaweed from being perfect! Love is mysteriously intangible! The *Jelly Beans in Life* can be sweet, provided the mixture of the rainbow colors does not tangle the seaweed in the mind! Larry was steadfastly in love with Susan, even though at times he detected not a gram of sweetness within her. Susan, on the other hand, had spent a lifetime attempting to dissect love and write a recipe that could be measured and quantified. She read volumes of poetry that attempted to do the same thing, but those attempts were also futile. She studied the lyrics of John Lennon, but even her hero did not convey any meaningful, concrete answers.

It was unlikely that Larry would ever be able to prove his devotion to Susan. No way to prove she was number one. Perhaps, if Charlie could speak, he'd be able to explain the mysteries of the *Jelly Beans in Life* to them.

The Schafers turned up Penny Lane and greeted a Charlie who was more frisky than usual. Susan exclaimed, "What's up, Charlie? Why in the world are you so excited?"

As Susan and Larry headed to the backdoor, they were again stopped dead in their tracks. On the porch was the mangled corpse of a rattlesnake. Charlie barked again as his tail wagged excitedly.

"Susan, it looks like Charlie got revenge. He just tied Papa's record of killing rattlers. That makes the score one to one!"

It was three o'clock. The meeting would start at five, but Susan wanted to get there early, ahead of the crowd. The council members would be on the stage with Mayor Sam, who would act as the chairman. Mary would be in attendance representing the press. The town hall meeting was advertised with posters all around town and there was an announcement in the *Gazette*. It was uncertain how many citizens would be present, but this kind of meeting typically attracted a handful. But, since the moratorium had become so controversial, a larger crowd was a possibility.

"Larry, I think you should stay home and take it easy."

"Not a chance. This is your big day, and I want to be there to support you!"

"Must you always be so contrary?"

"I have no idea what you're talking about!"

Larry replaced his bloody slacks with loose fitting shorts that would not bind or irritate the wound. His nicest Hawaiian shirt made him look respectable. He did not want to embarrass Susan on her big night!

Susan was dressed as if she were headed to the high school to teach

English. The combination of conservative and no nonsense suited her well. She wore no lipstick or perfume. The non-verbal message radiated 'proceed with caution'!

They were not the first to arrive at the high school. In fact, even Mayor Sam's '53 Chevy was in the parking lot. Obvious by its absence was Rex's black Cadillac. As Susan and Larry entered the auditorium, they greeted Kathleen, who was seated at a sign-up table that attendees would be unable to avoid.

"Hi, Kathleen. Glad to see your Corvair got you here. I arrived in Larry's Astro, so I know exactly what you go through. It's cause for celebration when the destination is actually reached!"

"Big night! I hope you put on some deodorant. Could be another high pressure system in the works. Will the reporter from the *Gazette* be here?"

"Without question!"

On the stage were chairs for each of the council members and a stool behind the podium for the mayor. An easel holding a king-sized tablet of paper almost as tall as Sam, was positioned handily.

Because Larry thought it best to fly way under the radar, he found a seat in the last row, to the side, and on the end. Susan walked up the steps to the podium where Blake and Jimmy were chatting with the mayor.

"So, what's the story on Rex?"

Mayor Sam handed Susan the letter of resignation he had received. "Looks like the three of you will decide the fate of the moratorium. Before we get started, I'd like each of you to tell me how you intend to vote. The choices are yes, no, or Plan 'S'."

"What's plan 'S'?", asked Jimmy.

"That's Susan's plan; the one we previously called Plan 'C'. I made an executive decision to rename it Plan 'S'!"

Blake spoke up, "I like Plan 'S'!"

Jimmy didn't hesitate, "Me too! It's a no-brainer!"

"Okay, Susan, what do you think?"

"I guess I'm outnumbered! Count me in!"

"Are all three of you fairly certain that your vote won't change?"

The three councilmen all confirmed their position.

"Okay, thank you. Let me complete my preparation."

The time was 4:30. Interested citizens would arrive soon. Susan turned to Blake and Jimmy, "Gentlemen, usually we sit on the stage like statues in a park when our neighbors walk in. Let's stand outside the door to greet them, and invite them in." It was agreed.

As the three Lake Mathias council members stood outside, activity in the parking lot gained momentum. At first, cars trickled in, but the trickle quickly became a stream, and then a flash flood. The majority of the town's people knew Susan, Blake, and Jimmy. There were jabs from parents who wanted to know why their child received a 'C' in Mrs. Schafer's English class. Several people asked Jimmy to call them about a potential remodel. Inquiries about home values were a very popular topic for Blake. Others asked where Rex was. Typically, the auditorium only saw this level of activity for a graduation.

Mary Wilson was a late arrival. "Hi Mary, Kathleen has a table set up for coffee and cookies. I'm drinking my coffee black!"

"Under the circumstances, that's probably a good idea!"

As five o'clock approached, a man wearing a blue sport coat and red tie entered. He introduced himself as Louis Woods, president of Cedar Wood Development.

As Mary found her seat, Jimmy kicked the door stop and began closing the door but a foot from outside blocked the door from closing. It was Rex. "Hello Jimmy. Great night for a big meeting, isn't it?" Jimmy shook Rex's outstretched hand.

Rex turned to Susan and commented, "And, it looks like the queen of the council is here! I'm certain that it pleases your majesty that I'm attending the coronation!"

The gears in Susan's mind spun as she searched for a scathing verbal ping pong play that Rex would be unable to return. Instead, she made the unexpected soft play to the middle of the table. "Oh, Rex, it is so wonderful to see you! Thank you so very much for attending!"

Rex stood, as if paralyzed, while the imaginary ball one-hopped gently off his belly.

Rex and Larry had met, but only briefly, at Sal's around Christmas. Rex took Larry's tactic of finding a seat away from the action. As he climbed down the steps, he didn't recognize the back of Larry's square head. He chose a seat on the end just two rows ahead of Larry. As Rex turned to sit down, Larry thought that it might be Rex, but he wasn't sure.

A moment later, Red sneaked in the back door and sat next to Larry. "Hi there, Ratchet! I'm here to watch Mrs. Ratchet hold court. My, oh my, looks like the whole damn town is here!"

Susan, followed by Blake and Jimmy, formed a procession and headed for their seat on the stage. Mayor Sam, dressed in his traditional red suspenders, began the meeting. After leading the 'Pledge of Allegiance', he got down to the business at hand. As usual, he was comfortable and amazingly calm.

"Citizens of Lake Mathias, I'm delighted to address this town hall meeting this 29th day of July, 1987. It's my pleasure to serve you, the citizens of this wonderful town. Your distinguished elected town council members are also present. They are seated to my left. Council members, as I call your name, please stand. Blake Parker. Jimmy Ray. Susan Schafer."

There was scattered applause akin to the fanfare a third string ball player receives when he enters a one sided game. The mayor continued, "I'm sure you're wondering why there are only three council members up here on the stage. Our fourth elected councilman, Rex Fisher, has tendered his resignation. Given the enormous salary and benefits that both the mayor and the council members are paid, Rex's resignation was quite a shock!"

The town's people, knowing that the mayor and councilmen were volunteers, chuckled.

"We're indebted to Rex, Blake, Jimmy, and Susan for their unselfish dedication to serve you, the people."

A hand raised in the audience. When Sam didn't acknowledge the questioner, town person yelled out. "Mr. Mayor, Mr. Mayor, why did Rex resign?"

"That's a very good question. That question should probably be answered, but it won't be answered by the mayor. Perhaps the man that resigned will answer it?"

The citizen continued, "There have been articles in the *Riverside Gazette* that suggest Rex was forced out. Will you speak to that?"

"The only comment I'll make is that Rex served the council well during his tenure. Neither I, nor any of the council members, asked Rex to resign. That was his choice. But again, I remind you that being a town council member is a tough job that requires an incredible commitment. The blood, sweat, and tears that are byproducts of the job take a toll on people both professionally and personally. Sometimes those pressures result in personal decisions that are not fair for us to judge. And, I'll remind you: these positions are as volunteer servants."

The crowd was not necessarily happy with Mayor Sam's comments, but accepted them. A squirming Rex sat in the back, undetected, except by the other council members and Larry. At one point, Rex stood up, as if to speak, but stopped himself and sat back down.

Mayor Sam put the meeting back on track. "So, my fellow citizens, let me move things along and explain some ground rules. Tonight, the council will be voting on the disposition of the moratorium that ends on July 31st. The mayor only votes if there is a tie. Unless there is an abstention, it will be unnecessary for the mayor to vote tonight. Also, for your information, the council is unanimous in their support of Plan 'S' proposed by Councilman Schafer. As you all know, I'm a retired educator. Henceforth, I'm more comfortable talking to you at this easel with a marking pen. I was not expecting this big a crowd. I hope you folks in the back will be able to see what I'm writing."

Sam wrote down the three choices available to the council.

"Option one is a 'yes' to continue the moratorium that allows a maximum of twenty-six houses to be built annually. Option two is to vote 'no' on the moratorium and allow unregulated building. Then, there's Plan 'S' introduced by Councilman Schafer, which would increase building substantially but attach a 5% fee to the builders doing the building. So, ladies and gentlemen, let me make this very easy for you."

Sam drew a line through options one and two.

"After much deliberation, the council has determined that options one and two are not viable for our town. They are unofficially dead. The council, tonight is poised to vote for option 'S'. The discussion we are inviting is the implementation of Plan 'S'. The hope is that our town, living on stone soup today will be serving beef stew tomorrow. Down the road, after Plan 'S' is actually successful, the town of Lake Mathias may have money to budget and be rejuvenated. No, we're not asking the town to actually pay us for the work we do."

A hand went up in the audience. "How much money are we talking about?"

"The new ruling will allow almost five times as much building as we've had: fifty units on one acre lots and twenty-five units each on two and one half, five, and ten acre parcels. That's a total of 125 units."

Sam wrote the information on the board. "Time will tell how much money will actually be generated by this proposed plan. I'll leave it to you folks to do your own math. Obviously there are lots of variables and few givens, but any way you slice it, our town will be way ahead of anywhere we ever dreamed we could be. The actual accounting, of course, will be made public for all of you to see, review, and perhaps scrutinize. Five percent of a small number is, of course, a relatively small number. Five percent of a large number would generate a fair amount of money that could transform this town into something really special!"

Even though the mayor went to great lengths to say almost nothing, most of the town's folks seemed to be happy. It was becoming evident to the majority, that the implementation of Plan 'S' could only help the town, certainly not harm it. A jittering wave from the builder with the red tie got the mayor's attention.

"Mr. Mayor, my name is Louis Woods. I'm here representing Cedar Wood Development. I believe you and the council are making some assumptions that may not be in the best interest of Lake Mathias. Number one, the cavalier rejection of the provision that would open up building to free enterprise is puzzling. Who can deny that Sunnymeade, the town to your east, has prospered from allowing un-regulated growth? As for your 5% fee on a regulated quantity of building on regulated lot sizes, there will be a very short list of builders remotely interested in that proposition. The 'S' option is nothing short of extortion!"

The mayor calmly stayed in control. "Thank you very much, Mr. Woods. Sunnymeade has certainly grown in spectacular fashion. No one can argue that point. Let me ask the people here if their vision for Lake Mathias is to become the next Sunnymeade. Please stand up if it is your dream for this town to be the next Sunnymeade."

Louis Woods and Rex Fisher were the only ones to stand.

"Now please stand if you favor the 'S' Plan."

There were a handful of abstainers, the rest of the crowd stood firm and tall.

Another hand went up. "Mrs. Schafer. It sounds like this Plan 'S' is your idea. It sounds like a plan that is good for everyone. Builders get to build, growth will not be out of control, and the town will get a blood transfusion. How did you develop this plan?"

"Thank you very much for asking such a great question. And thank you all for being here tonight. I, like many of you who live in town, love our small town feel. On the other hand, we are kind of dying because we just don't have the money for things like ballfields, equestrian trails, and parks. My husband Larry and I had breakfast with a friend of his. In the discussion about the moratorium, he suggested it might be in the town's best interest to meet the truck half-way. That was the origin of the compromise that has just been laid out so eloquently by our mayor."

A smart question followed, "Who takes care of the money?"

Mayor Sam addressed the question squarely, "Great question! I don't believe that either the mayor or the town council should be charged with that responsibility. It will likely be in the best interest of the townspeople to hire a part time treasurer with impeccable credentials and integrity. The revenue generated from the building fees would fund that person's salary."

Another hand went up. "With all due respect, how can, we the people, be assured that there will not be 'shenanigans' in play between the builders and the town council. If this 'S' proposal has the impact that is hoped for, there may be competition between builders to get those permits. We know that both Blake and Jimmy have ties to real estate. And it seems to me that Rex's resignation on the eve of this new proposal has the smell of something being swept under the rug."

Susan quickly responded, "Thank you for your very insightful comment and question. It's true that politics on both national and local levels have had their share of controversies. The system works best when there is community involvement. Based on the turnout tonight, we certainly have that. Thank you all for being here with your neighbors, your elected council, and, of course, our wonderful mayor. The press is also here to gather first-hand information so that it can be reported to the community as a whole. Let me introduce you to Mary Wilson, who is covering the moratorium for the *Riverside Gazette*. Mary will you please stand and tell us how it is that you are covering this critical issue."

"My editor assigned this story to me. It seems that a council woman, named Susan Schafer, suggested the *Gazette* report to its readers the disposition of the moratorium."

"Thank you, Mary. We all look forward to reading about it in tomorrow's *Gazette*. It has been my hope to get everyone involved by publicizing the pertinent information. If the intent was to 'pull a quick one', getting the media involved, certainly, would not have been prudent. As for Blake, he is a well-respected realtor in town and Jimmy is a custom builder with an impeccable track record. Both of them rely on their reputation to make a living. No one is perfect, but these gentlemen, who you, the citizens elected, are as solid as they come. And then, there's our beloved Mayor Sam. The only way he ever measures anything is by asking one simple question, 'Are we doing the right thing?' So, in closing, I'm very proud to be associated with these men. Let me assure you, this council always has the townspeople's best interest in mind!"

"How about Rex Fisher?"

"Since he's no longer a member of the council, I have no comment!"

A voice from the back of the auditorium announced, "Hi, I'm Rex Fisher."

There was an eerie silence as Rex continued, "I'm no longer a member of the council. I resigned because of a potential conflict of interest. I'm a retired fireman who is currently employed by The Workers Union on a part time basis. Labor unions have helped many families in this country get a 'fair shake'. It's a documented fact that The Workers Union owns buildable property in town. My intentions have always been honorable, but it became obvious that some of you might think there was a conflict of interest, so, I resigned. I must also say that I did have a conflict with Susan Schafer, who is a labor union hater. If, in fact, there was a conflict of interest for me, a conflict of interest certainly exists for Susan Schafer!"

Susan felt the pain of Rex's snakelike bite. In one split second the high pressure system returned, just as Kathleen had predicted. Two rattlesnake bites in one day were tough to endure, but she was up for the fight.

"Mr. Fisher, thank you for your much anticipated participation. I'd like to set the record straight, and once I've done that, I'll ask you, the citizens, if you're compelled to ask me to resign from the council. If you are so inclined, I'll do so gladly. First of all, I'm neither union member nor union hater. It is true that, for personal reasons, I'm the only teacher at Lake Mathias High School that does not belong to the teacher's union.

"The fact of the matter is that I did belong to the teacher's union. In fact, I was the union representative for this high school. During my tenure, the teachers in the district went on strike. That, for me, was awkwardly demeaning. There I was, a professional educator carrying a placard, when all I really wanted to do was to watch the reaction of children when I turned a light bulb on in their heads. After spending a miserable day picketing, I made the decision to either quit teaching or quit the union. I think you know what my decision was. Do I hate all unions? No. Did I hate being in a union? Yes. If not wanting to be in a labor union compels you the people of Lake Mathias to ask for my resignation, please, let me know now."

As Susan was given a standing ovation, Mayor Sam stepped forward from the podium. "Ladies and Gentlemen, I think you can see that the town is in good hands. We'll now make it official. Councilman Blake Parker, how do you vote?"

Blake was loud and firm, "I vote for Plan 'S'!"

"Councilman Jimmy Ray, how do you vote?"

"I vote for the Susan Shafer option!"

"And last, but certainly not least, Councilman Susan Schafer, how do you vote?"

"Mr. Mayor, "I'm voting for Plan 'S' because it meets the truck half-way!"

That comment triggered yet another standing ovation.

Rex never heard the sound of either ovation. As Susan uttered the last word of her defense, he stormed out of the auditorium followed by Larry and Red, who escorted him to his car. Louis Woods went out of his way to shake the hands of the councilmen and the mayor. He knew in months and years to come, that he would need to befriend them. He knew that Cedar Wood Development would be an aggressive builder in Lake Mathias, even if it cost 5% to participate.

There was a giant celebration at Sal's following the biggest town hall meeting that Lake Mathias had ever experienced. The mayor, Jimmy, Blake, and Susan were all there. Kathleen, followed by a trail of oil, also attended. Mary Wilson, Red, and, of course, Larry were eager participants!

Sal served hot dogs, potato salad, and lemonade.

Susan made sure she hugged everyone. The mayor and Red each received two hugs. Larry got the big prize, a kiss that sucked the sting of the rattlesnake bite right out his square head.

Red couldn't resist, "You are quite a kisser, Mrs. Ratchet!"

Mary turned to Red. "Jumping bullfrogs, here's a kiss for you. Thanks for convincing Susan to meet the truck half-way!"

Red was both surprised and elated. "Wow that was the sweetest kiss I can remember!"

Mary responded passionately, "That's because I drink my coffee with a splash of milk to make me smile and a sprinkle of sugar to make me sweet!"

Red was so happy, you would have thought he was in Ventura.

Mayor Sam pulled on his red suspenders, took a sip of Sal's iced cold lemonade, and smiled.

Susan turned to Larry. "You broke your record!"

"What record?"

"I saw you and Red escort Rex out. You've now done two nice things in a row for me. Do you want to increase the streak to three?"

Larry, as usual was confused. Before he could respond, Susan continued, "Will you still need me, will you still feed me, when I'm sixty-four?"

Larry's square head shone like the brightest lantern on a moonless Lake Mathias night. "Only, if you'll have some jelly beans with me!"

ACKNOWLEDGEMENTS

This book would not be possible without the help of my team of "BOOK BUDDIES" who inspire me, keep me straight, and roll up their sleeves when I need help. This teamwork ensures my books are the best they can be. My hope is that I've created a literary keepsake that readers enjoy and recommend to others.

Beverly Schmalhofer
Chief Editor who keeps me grounded

Patti Plummer
MGA2

Joe Notte
MGA2

Carrie and Peggy @ Author's Marketing Experts
Marketing wizards that connect readers to my books

Mike and Linda Edmonds
Pre-readers and this author's biggest fans

Bruce Carnevale
Industry Consultant

Bob Russak
A Jelly Beans fan who guides me through legalities

Lisa Rogal
Facebook administrator

Dan Rogal
Website Designer

Andrea Douglas
Administrator

Mike Bowerman
Chapter artwork for Jelly Beans in Life

Arron Sanders
Amazon connection